Keisha & Trigga RELOADED

A Gangster Love Story

2

A NOVEL BY

LEO SULLIVAN
PORSCHA STERLING

JOIN OUR MAILING LIST!

SYNOPSIS

Keisha & Trigga are back for the long-awaited finale to this gangsta love series.

The pressure for Trigga is at an all-time high after Keisha is attacked while pregnant with their child. Not knowing whether his wife or unborn child will survive, Trigga tries to find the one he thinks is responsible for putting his family in danger. But being away from the streets for so long has him slipping in ways that could cost the ones closest to him their lives. Will he be able to get back on his feet in time to set things right and get his revenge?

Lania came to New York City with one goal: to help her children's father and Texas drug kingpin, Austin, to put into his place his plan to extort Trigga. But after working so closely with Trigga, she realizes that he, not Austin, may actually be the perfect thug to match her ride-or-die swag. But little can be hidden from Austin and when he finds out that Lania is getting much closer to Trigga than he required of her, he puts out a threat on her life and sets his sights on giving her the same end that he has in place for Trigga. But Lania knows if she can win Trigga's heart, she would earn not only his love but also his protection. Only Keisha lies in her way but Lania has never been one to say no to a challenge and Keisha is just an obstacle she'll have pleasure in removing.

Keisha & Trigga have managed to survive the threats of the streets in the past and cling on to their love. But this time it isn't only the streets that they are fighting against... other circumstances even have them fighting against each other. Will love win in the end?

ORDER OF THE KEISHA & TRIGGA SERIES

This book is dedicated to the readers who support Leo Sullivan Presents & Royalty Publishing House and the authors who make up each of those teams. We appreciate you.

1

___

The acoustic sounds droned on like a symphony of dreadful noises. There was an EKG machine to his left, and to his right was some type of mechanical breathing apparatus attached to Keisha's mouth and nose. Her face was so badly disfigured that she was unrecognizable, beaten black and blue. Both of her eyes were severely swollen closed, and her top lip was nearly the size of a baseball. She looked like the elephant man.

"Ohh, Gud," Trigga exclaimed, all choked up. This was too much for his soul to bear. It was like déjà vu all over again, only worse. This was the one thing he feared, which was that harm would come to his family, especially his beloved, Keisha. His heart pained, eyes misty, as a ball of emotions consumed him as he stared at her body.

It took everything in Trigga's power not to turn his head away from the horrific sight of seeing his wife's battered and bruised body, so he stared at the bottle of salient dripping from a tube going directly into an intravenous needle connected to her arm.

Suddenly, the door opened and in came the murmur of hospital sounds. A public announcement blared when in walked a doctor with blonde hair bespectacled with glasses, and a stethoscope was hanging from around his neck. His white scrubs were stained with what looked like blood. In his hand was a clipboard.

"Are you the patient's husband?" the doctor asked as the blatant sound of the breathing apparatus droned on endlessly.

"Yes. Is she going to make it, and what about the baby?" Trigga asked in a croaked voice.

The doctor licked his paper-thin lips and paused before he spoke, as he furrowed his brow.

With a subtle shrug, he began to speak slow and methodically.

"She is in a drug-induced coma to help reduce the swelling on her brain. I'll have to admit things are not looking too good for her. She has about a thirty-percent chance of survival, and as for the baby, the prognosis is worse. I am sorry," the doctor said with a grim expression, and began to adjust one of the instruments on the EKG machine.

"Oh fuck, man. God, no, not her and the baby. God must don't like me," Trigga said heartbroken, and pinched his eyes closed tight as he hung his head, holding onto the guardrail on the bed.

The sound of the doctor's shoes squeaked on the linoleum floors as he suddenly turned around and faced Trigga and put a comforting hand on his shoulder.

He asked in an authoritative voice, "Do you believe in God?"

Trigga nodded his head. "Yes, but it's a matter of does He believe in me. This is terrible. What kind of god let's a mother and her child die like this?" His voice cracked with emotion.

"That is not for us to judge. Just continue to pray and keep your faith," the doctor admonished congenially.

"Yeah... Yeah...okay, I'ma pray on it, Doc," Trigga said, and reached out and held Keisha's hand, gasping at what he saw. Three of her fingernails had been torn completely off, all the way to the core, and were red and bruised badly. It wouldn't have been so bad had it not been for the fact Keisha was a girly girl. Always had she prided herself on being meticulous about her fingernails and pedicure, and to see her hands like that really got to him.

His phone then chimed. He looked at the caller I.D.; it was Lania. Instantly, he became overwhelmed with a sense of relief, then dread, as he looked at his wife lying in bed in a coma. As she fought for her life, a feeling of trepidation hit him in the pit of his gut. The phone continued to ring. He stared at it, then cast a weary glance at his wife. The symphony of sound coming from the machines attached to her sounded like a caustic, sad song to his ears.

"Bae, I gotta take this call. I'ma be right back.... walkin' out into the hall-way," he said, speaking barely above a whisper that seemed to echo in his mind. There was no way in hell he was going to talk to another chick right in front of her; to him and their love, it felt like the ultimate betrayal.

"What's going on, Lania?" Trigga asked as he began to pace the halls as people walked by with smug expressions. To Trigga, hospitals were dreary places where people came to mourn for the sick and dying, and now he found himself in that same somber mood.

"I heard about what happened to your wife, Keisha. If you need anything, just let me know. I really do care for you."

"...Mmm, yeah. Uh... what's going on with the club?" he asked, avoiding her sentiments. The reality was, as much as he hated it, he really did enjoy her company at times. And not just that. The one time he had let her preform oral six on him, that was the best he had ever had his dick sucked in his life. Her head game was incredible; it was like she had a velvet tongue.

"That's what I want to talk to you about, too."

"What?"

"The club. I think Tory stole some money."

"What da fuck!?" Trigga scoffed just as an old lady that was getting pushed by a young attractive Black nurse crinkled her gnarly brew at him in disgust as she was being wheeled by. The nurse smiled at him flirtatiously and wiggled her ass in passing to get his attention, as she looked over her shoulder to make sure he was watching. He paid neither of them any mind as he stopped in front of an exit sign across from a vending machine.

"Yes, about nine hundred dollars, and I don't think this was the first time. The last time I replaced it with the tips I earned, but this time it was too much."

"Damn, fuckin' bitch! Are you sure?" he asked while balling his fist tight.

"Yes. When I was counting up the night's earnings from the bar, she brought in the money from the VIP section and told me it was sixteen thousand, but when I counted it, it was short nine hundred, and when I confronted her about it, she said it must have been Wahida's fault, the girl that bartends."

"That's bullshit! Wahida would never steal! I'ma fire that bitch as soon as I get there." Trigga was fuming hot, but there were other troubling matters he needed to tend to. One of them was his dying wife.

"I wanna see you again," she said in a sensuous voice that stirred at something deep in his loins, that place only a feminine touch could fill. But Trigga knew the virtues of a woman; a hot piece of pussy and some smoking head could also be the catalyst for his demise. "Never put your feelings into something that spreads apart, especially a stripper's ass," was the diction in his street savvy head. So he moved to dead that shit ASAP, especially with his wife lying only a few yards away fighting for her life along with an unborn child.

"Yo, shawtie, dig. That shit that happened the other day, how my dick ended up in your mouth, dat ain't gon' happen again, na'mean? 'Cause a nigga got a wife and family—"

"Nigga, stop. You know you liked it. Rarely does a nigga cum... twice... in my mouth."

"Umm...Just remember what I said. Keep this shit one hunnid on some business type shit—"

"That was my business to please you, even if I have to keep your dick all the way down the back of my throat and swallow them babies. Now, if you don't like it, you can fire me right now and I can have Tory run the club. I'm a stripper during a great economy; a bitch gon' find employment, even if I have to visit the Gentleman's Club, your competition, like the rest of your girls have been doing."

"Bitch, don't try me with that fuck shit!" Trigga retorted with a weak gambit like he didn't care, but the reality was the way she positioned herself at the club made her help invaluable. As much as he hated to admit it, if she left at this point in time, he had no one to trust to take her place.

"No, don't try me," she said tersely, then added, "I'll see you tonight. There is something I need to talk to you about."

"It better be business!" he snapped.

"It is; your business is my pleasure," she said jovially.

Then something dawned on him. It was something she had mentioned earlier.

"What you mean by the rest of the girls going to the Gentleman's Club. Is Red working there?" he asked, and there was a pregnant pause that alarmed him. It took her too long to answer.

"Uhh, no, no!" she responded.

"How you know then?" he shot back. "You must have been in there."

"...No...no, Trigga, don't be silly. I just heard people talking—"

"Who you heard talking? Shit falling apart. I'm here in this fuckin' hospital, my wife is fighting for her life, and it sounds like you're talking in riddles n'shit!!" he said flustered, making a mental note to go check out the Gentleman's Club. Something didn't feel right with Lania and he just couldn't put his finger on it.

"It's just gossip; nothing big, really. If it was, I would have told you. And my heart goes out to you and your wife. I'm so happy you got your boy back.

I can't wait to see you tonight," she cooed in a seductive voice. Still, something wasn't right; he could feel it on his skin.

"Nia, if I find out there is some shady shit going on, it's going to be a problem!"

"What are you talkin' about?" Her voice screech at a high octave that again gave more reason to his suspicions.

CLICK!

He hung the phone up in her face. That night when the Gentleman's Club opened, he intended to be there front and center, but he would never be prepared for what happened next.

"*B*itch, what the fuck with all this lovey dovey shit!" Austin said as he walked back into the room. He was wearing only his boxer shorts and socks. His brawny, masculine chest, sculptured like a work of art, was covered in tattoos. He hauled off and slapped the shit out of her, hitting her so hard one of the tracks in her hair came off, along with her earring. She hadn't heard him walk back into the room and didn't know how long he had been standing there. He had left to go get some more coke to roll up a "dirty." The only way he could smoke his loud was laced with cocaine.

"What you hit me for?" she cried out, as she rubbed the large handprint welt on the side of her face like it was on fire.

"Bitch, I heard you talkin' 'bout you sucked his dick and he came twice or some shit like that." Austin was irate, exasperated so much his nostrils flared. He thought about punching her like a man. As he stood in his boxers, his dick was partially hanging out without him even noticing it.

"No! No! Baby, I only did as you said. I called him and dick teased him. I said only one man had cum in my mouth twice. I was talking about you—"

WHAM!

He slapped her again, this time harder. "Bitch, you fucking lying!" he said, testing her.

The truth was, he couldn't be for sure what she had exactly said because he wasn't really paying attention. He was high as fuck and expertly rolling the blunt, trying not to waste the cocaine. The reality was he also felt like she was catching feelings for the nigga, Trigga, and that was definitely not part of the game plan. The other issue was Lania was a pain freak, a masochist. In her own weird, perverted way, she actually liked getting her ass whipped and being abused sexually, and in other ways, it wasn't uncommon for Austin to bring women home in the wee hours of the night, high off coke, and demand that Lania be part of a threesome with her sucking dick and eating pussy. Once, Austin had shoved the neck of a beer bottle up her vagina and his dick up her ass as the other girl licked the streaming beer cascading out of her vagina.

Being a stripper, enticing men with the sexy allure of her audacious body, was a bonus to her.

He set the blunt down on the nightstand and violently grabbed her around her throat, with so much force, it lifted her off her feet and slammed her into the wall as the table next to the bed came crashing down.

"Bitch... Don't fuckin' play with me!" He choked harder as veins began to protrude from the side of her head. He was cutting off her windpipe, and at the same time, causing her to receive multiple orgasms.

"Ugh... I wasn't lying... I, ughhh... did what you said. He... asked about the Gentleman's Club...Red..."

"Whaat!?" He let her go and she plummeted to the floor, gasping for air on her knees, and looked up. His ten-inch dick was ramrod hard and wavering like a flagpole with each subtle movement. Truth be told, he enjoyed whipping her ass just as much as she liked getting her ass whipped. The only bad thing is that she had to go and mention Red's name. She was the stripper that had helped set up the lick that got B.J. killed. Now she worked at the Gentleman's Club and had changed her name to Goddess to elude Trigga. Austin had been totally against it, but what could he do? The bitch was a stripper and a cokehead; he'd only paid her an eight-ball of coke and a thousand dollars. The reality was, she was an addict with a habit and a trade. She stripped to earn a living and to supply her expensive high.

"Fuck. I know we should have killed that bitch after the caper. How the fuck he find out?" Austin asked as his dick began to shrink in size like an inner tube with a hole in it.

"I dunno." She feigned innocence as she continued to gasp to catch her breath. From somewhere in another section of the house, a baby cried and there was the sound of children frolicking throughout the house.

"What did he say?!" Austin asked while he continued to stand over her with his massive dick shrinking smaller and smaller, and his masculine chest heaved with each breath. She glanced up at him, dick only inches from her face, and for some reason, her mouth began to water as she resisted the urge not to reach out and touch him, to stroke him. Besides, he had his fists balled tightly. She enjoyed a good ass whipping, minus the black eyes and fractured ribs. She was tired of telling people she had been in a bad car accident and the car hydroplaned, when they asked what happened to her.

"He...he... he just said it out the blue; said he was going to go to the club and look for her."

"Bitch, you stuttering and some mo' shit; fuck you lying 'bout?"

WHAM!

He slapped her so hard, spit flew from her mouth. She was seeing stars in flashing neon light colors.

"I ain't lying." She reached out and grabbed him around his lower waist. His dick against her face and the heat of her mouth was salacious as her hot tears fell, staining his boxers. She still was in the danger zone as she pressed her face harder against him.

"Bitch, you is fucking lying!" he yelled, and she could feel his body coil, stiffening like he was about to deliver the next blow with his fist to the side of her face, next to her eye.

"Nooo! Nooo! I wouldn't lie to you," she wailed.

Just as he reached back to strike her—one of the hazards of loving a ruthless thug as a baby daddy—there was an intrusive knock at the door. He cringed, aggravated.

"Who the fuck is it?"

"Dadda, we hungreee, and Shelly boo booed and peed on herself." Their seven-year-old son, Jamel, whined through the door. Truth be told, Austin never really liked the boy, and it was no secret. He and Lania had broken up and got back together, and the timing was suspicious. Also, the fact the boy was red with freckles and looked nothing like either parent didn't help the situation.

"It's some fuckin' cereal in the kitchen. Eat dat. Yo' mama coming out in a minute. And I'ma whip your ass again if you knock on dat fuckin' do' one more time."

As he talked, Lania stole the opportunity to sling his limp dick in her mouth like it was a large wet noodle, and sucked on it wantonly as if she was starved and hadn't had a meal in weeks.

"...But we had cereal last night for dinner," his son whined.

"Fuck 'way from the do'. I told you, I'ma beat your ass..." His words suddenly came out minced as he glanced down to see Lania sucking his dick at jack hammer speed, as she masterfully masturbated him and manipulated his balls, stroking him delicately with her fingernails, and spit on the head, then slurped up his entire dick all the way to the helm, pushing it down the back of her throat.

Damnn... Sh...sh... shit," he groaned, feeling his toes curl.

This bitch know she can suck a dick, he thought to himself. *But she also think a nigga stupid.*

He suddenly grabbed a handful of her weave and slapped the shit out of her.

"Ouch!" She complained and looked up at him, a sliver of saliva dangling off her lubricious bottom lip, and it turned him on in a way that he couldn't understand as his dick dangled solitarily, devoid of her mouth.

"Bitch, you wanna have all the sense, think a nigga slow. I should beat your muthufuckin' ass black and blue again for trying me with that fuck shit!"

"I didn't do nothing," she complained and put his dick back in her mouth and sucked on it with ferocity, while jacking him off, licking up and down his long shaft, then feasted on his balls. The sound echoed, resonating throughout the house.

There was another knock at the door. They both ignored it as he grabbed her by her hair again; only this time, he intentionally shoved his dick as far as it would go down the back of her throat, causing her to gag and choke, her eyes instantly filling with tears, a ball of snot running off her nose.

"Bitch, suck this dick. I'ma bust three nuts in your fuck ass mouth and set a new record, then we going to the Gentleman's Club to get that bitch, Red. I need for you to kill that bitch and it's a wrap. She knows too much, and if Trigga gets to her first, we got a real problem 'cause she will tell him about me and that you're working with me."

All Lania could do was nod her head obediently "yes" and hope it didn't take him all day to bust a nut. She needed her energy to meet with Trigga, and she didn't want her face all messed up, or to be too tired. She planned on sucking his dick too, or maybe something kinkier. Like, maybe she could seduce him into hitting her in her ass, that was if he didn't get to Red first. Austin was right, they did need to silence Red and as quickly as possible.

Then Austin suddenly reached down and pinched her nipple so hard it made her scream in agony. He then shoved his dick further down her throat and smacked the shit out of her again. On the nightstand, he retrieved his "dirty blunt" and fired it up, and blew a palm of smoke at her, then shoved his dick in and out of her mouth. Just that fast he was about to cum, and he did. With a long stream of milky white, he painted her face as his body shivered, then he shoved his dick back in her mouth.

"Eat up all dat dick, bitch; all twelve inches!!" He chuckled. "One nut down, two more to go! I need for you to swallow them shits," he said and slapped her again. The pain never felt so good. Lania had an orgasm that ran down her leg, saturating the floor, and that only seemed to excite her more. She began to suck his dick at jack hammer speed. All the while, she was thinking about Trigga.

"Punk bitch, go over there and pass me that pile of coke on the dresser."

"I thought you said you was going to slow down on snorting coke," she said in a small voice.

"I am, when they stop making it," he retorted, and slapped her on her ass so hard it left a handprint. The sensation felt so good, her pussy squirted cum, and a seismic shiver ran down her spine as she wiggled her ass intentionally as she paddled over and snatched the plate of coke off the dresser.

"Put dat shit on the head of my dick and rub it off," he commanded as he began to stroke himself.

Now she had a problem. "I'on know. The last time you asked me to do that when we were in Texas, your dick stayed hard all day and my jowls got tired."

Phew!

He slapped her ass again and snatched the coke out her hand then yanked her down to her knees. "Just do what da fuck I say!" he snapped, and she obeyed. But secretly, as she rubbed the coke on the head of his dick, all she could think about was Trigga, and that made her horny as fuck while she primed his dick with the coke.

"Okay, I'ma suck the shit outta this dick, Trig—" She slipped and almost called him Trigga. And Austin was on her in a flash. He grabbed her around the throat with his large hands.

"Bitch, wha-da-fuck you just call me?!"

"Ughgg, ughgg, you choking.... meeee." She gurgled words like she was being dunked under water, drowning.

"Fuck you just said, bitch?" he choked harder.

"I said... I'ma suck dat dick bigger... like I always do, and make the head swell big." She struggled to talk as his grip suddenly loosened around her neck and he let off on her, causing her to expel a deep wind like she had been holding her breath for minutes.

"See, that is why I hate for you to snort coke. You be trippin' and shit, acting all paranoid," she said, rubbing her throat, still trying to get her wind back.

"Aw, bitch, you be loving 'dis dope dick," Austin said, and snorted a line of coke then shoved Lania's head back down on his dick. Secretly, she liked it; the passion and pain. She imagined it was Trigga's dick in her mouth.

3

"Come on, Cam. I'ma need for you to be a big boy." Trigga tried to persuade his son as he stood in the living room of the babysitter's house.

"I wanna go with you and Mommy! You said I could go last time, and I ain't seen my mommy, and you never came back like you said. I want my mommy!!" Cam cried pensively. The elderly lady, Ms. Jackson, who was in her fifties, was the child's babysitter, and tried to do everything in her power to soothe the boy, but nothing would work.

"I'ma come back and get you this time and you gon' come home with Daddy, I promise," Trigga pleaded with his heart on his sleeve.

"But I want my mommy tooooo." He bawled, crying, with his little shoulders hunched and rolling, full of heartache and despair, as tears streaked his handsome face.

"I told you we gon' see her soon."

"When!? I want my mommy... I want my mommy." The child continued to cry as he shoved away from his dad, and for the first time in Trigga's life, he saw something that Keisha had always said. "That boy just like you with his temperament." And there was no denying it that time. Trigga squatted down to eye level and attempted to plea bargain with his beloved son.

"Cam... I promise, I'ma come back soon, and you're going to see mom; that's my word, little nigga."

"NO! I don't want you to leave! And I want my mommy!!!" He broke down again and Trigga just happened to look up and see Ms. Jackson staring with her eyes full of tears. Something tugged at his chest when he looked back down at his child, and he scooped him up in his arms in a loving embrace.

"Cam, come on, man, stop crying. Please stop crying, lil' man... I need for you to be a big boy. Daddy going through some shit. I'ma need for you to be a big boy. I don't never ask you this unless it's important," Trigga said, and swallowed the lump in his throat as he held his son at arm's length, and the two of them just stared at each other, and instantly, the boy's shoulders heaved. He sucked back his tears and hugged his daddy, and Trigga did the same. The old woman watched, astonished. It was an emotional moment. She actually turned her head away. She felt guilty, as if she were looking at something too personal.

Young love portrayed between a father and son.

"Okay, Daddy... I'ma be a big boy, but don't leave me here... I don't wanna be here, I wanna go with you and Mommy."

"I'll take you to Chuck E. Cheese, and I got you a new tablet with Spider Man cartoons. Just hang in there for me, lil' nigga, and let me deal with this. I need for you to be a big boy, my lil' man. Okay?"

"Okay... but when you comin' back, and where is my Spider-Man tablet?" The boy pouted but was determined to muster up the courage to suck it up for the sake of his dad.

"Right here."

Trigga reached into his backpack that also held a Glock sixteen-shot .9mm, along with a Tec-9 fully loaded with a hundred-round clip, moved his weapons of warfare to the side and then handed his son his toy.

Afterwards, with Cameron poised on the couch playing with his favorite game, Ms. Jackson walked Trigga to the front door.

The old woman admonished sternly, "That boy gon' need some help, you hear me? He's having nightmares and peeing in the bed. You young folks is too much. I've been babysitting that boy since he was two and this has nevah happened," she said, and crossed her arms over her large bosoms.

"I know it's hard on him, but what do I tell him? His mama in a coma and might die," Trigga said begrudgingly.

"What you needs ta'do is spend more time with the child."

"I am... I mean, I'm trying—"

"How is dat!? Few days ago, the boy was kidnapped, and Lord knows what else happened."

"No, that was just somebody trying to prove a point."

"Child, is you serious? What kind of way is that to prove a point by using an innocent baby? Y'all young folks kill me these days," she chided him.

All Trigga could do was hang his head; the old woman had a point.

"And what you doin' with them guns n' stuff in your bag?" she asked, as her eyes held contempt. She must have peeped the guns when he looked into his backpack for the tablet. He was going to make up a quick lie, but the old woman was sharp, so instead, he decided to tell the truth than risk the ridicule.

"I got 'em to protect myself."

She frowned. "Protect yourself from what, an army?"

Trigga would have laughed despite the situation, but instead, he grabbed the doorknob to make his quick exit. He was no match for the old woman and he knew it.

"Just take care of him and I'ma come back tomorrow and pick him up," he said with a stiff chin, resisting the urge to look at her.

"Humph... How about you come back tonight and take him to school. He would like that very much."

Trigga lost it. To him it sounded like the lady was accusing him of not being a good dad. He raised his voice. "I toldja the boy was abducted from school, and I can't come back tonight. I'm having trouble with my club, damn. If you don't wanna keep him, just say it, and I can find somebody else..." Trigga's words got lost in his throat as he looked at the frail old woman. She suddenly took a timid step back and cringed at him apprehensively as her hand eased into her housecoat pocket for whatever she had stashed there to defend herself.

"Now you knows you's ain't just gon' talk to me no any kinda way, young man."

"I...I'm sorry... Please, can you keep him for me? I don't have nobody else," Trigga said, talking to his reflection in the screen-door glass. He didn't trust himself to look directly in her face. She would possibly be able to tell he was a mere husk of his former self. The intentions of trying to do too much was taking a toll on him.

"Yeah, sure, but if you's ever raise your voice at me like that again, I's gone cut you from asshole to appetite, you hear me?" she threatened with a glimmer of giddiness on her wrinkled mahogany face. In her pocket was a straight razor, the old-school kind barbers used to give shaves with.

"Yes, ma'am," Trigga responded in a husky voice, as he continued to stare out the door.

"Now you be careful."

"Yes, ma'am."

With that, Trigga walked out the door. The damp breeze felt good on his hot skin. He hadn't bathed or changed clothes in two days. His mind was on his woman and the culprit that had kidnapped his son then was bold enough to return him. The whole thing was madness and so uncharacteristic of how gangstas normally extort their victims. Something was wrong and he couldn't put his finger on it, but at least he had his son back. Now, all he needed was for Keisha to pull through this. On 25th Street, he stopped at a traffic light and reflected back on the last forty-eight hours of his life, and his mind flashed back on the horrific sight of his beloved Keisha lying in a hospital room fighting for her life.

"Fuck!" He slammed his fist onto the dashboard. That was when the car behind him began to blatantly honk its horn. The light had turned green and Trigga had not realized it. His mind was in a daze. Just as he pulled off, the car behind him sped up. It was an old ancient van, possibly a work vehicle. The occupant raised down the window and gave Trigga the middle finger. He was a young white dude, *eager to get his ass whipped*, Trigga thought as he stared back. They stopped at another red light at an intersection, and the guy pulled up next to Trigga in the raggedy van.

"Hey, you, black boy, you got a problem... Fuck you looking over here for?" the guy taunted as he waved a large crowbar of some type. That was when Trigga realized it was about three white guys in the van; two in the front seat and possibly more in the back, and they were trying to get at him. Road rage was at an all-time high in New York; this was far from being uncommon.

Trigga calmly reached into his backpack for the .9mm, and eased down the window, aiming the gun. "Yeah, fuck ass cracka, I got a problem. I don't like white BOYS that think they tough."

"Fuck youuuuu..." the driver said and ducked behind the steering wheel and sped off. For a fleeting moment, he actually fumed and considered giving chase. Then suddenly, his phone chimed and he hoped it the hospital calling to tell him that Keisha was going to be okay and he could come get her.

His heart sank when he looked at the caller I.D. and realized the number that was calling was coming from a blocked number. Just when he was about to ignore it, his better judgment told him to answer it anyway. Besides, it still might be from the hospital. It wasn't unusual for organizational phone numbers to come up blocked on his phone.

"Hello?" For some reason, his heart beat fast just as an eighteen-wheeler passed, honking its horn; he was almost hit.

"Yo, my nigga, wuz good?" a raspy voice said on the other end of the phone. The voice sounded eerily familiar.

"Who the fuck is this?" Trigga returned. He had no times for games.

"I'm the nigga that you owe that money to. I gave you back your son on the strength, beat your wife's ass on the brink of death, and made sure she would need reconstructive surgery just to prove a point to you," the voice bragged.

"ME!?"

Trigga swerved, cutting off another car, and pulled over to the side of the road. He held the phone so tight his knuckles cracked when he yelled into the phone.

"When I find out who the fuck this is, I'ma cut your balls off and kill you real slow. You gon' die, fuck nigga, and that's on err'thang I love. When I find you—"

"Hold up, partner, is that any kind of way to talk to a nigga that saved your child? I could have cut off some fingers and sent them shits in a box to show you I wasn't playin' with'cha bitch ass, but instead, I let him go, even though you tried a nigga, thinking I was going to just walk into an ambush." The voice on the other end chuckled derisively in a way that made Trigga's flesh crawl, and not just that; there was something sinister about the voice, and he was sure he had heard it before. It was the same voice of the gunman that had robbed him and killed J.B.—he was certain of it. For the first time in his life, he felt a timorous shiver run down his spine as fear gripped deep in his gut.

Where do I know him from? Trigga's mind churned.

"So here is the deal, my nigga. This how we rockin' from this point on. You gon' have to double up on the money now since you tried me with that country ass slick Willie shit."

"Double up? Man, I don't have that kind of money," Trigga said, his voice giving way to concerns.

"Oh, you can find it. Why don't you ask Queen? I see she fucks with you hard."

Trigga took the phone away from his ear and looked at it in scrutiny as he frowned, and his temper got the best of him when he growled into the phone.

"Fuck nigga, who is YOU!?"

"I'm your worst nightmare, nigga, and so far, I have continued to do everything that I promised, but I spared you last time. I promise you, next time, I'ma make sure you dress up for funerals; twin caskets type of shit if you don't stay with the game plan."

Frustrated, Trigga actually felt a pang of dread and utter despair. Whoever this formidable foe was, he was a force to be reckoned with. Trigga collapsed on the steering wheel with his eyes closed tight as if it would help chase away the demons in his mind and the virulent voice on the other end of the phone. Emphatically, he began to rant on the phone. With thoughts of his wife, he banged his mighty fist on the dashboard.

"God, man, what have I done to you? Why the fuck is you torturing me, tormenting me and my family? You put my fucking wife in the hospital. You doing too much, man. Actions have consequences."

"You right, yo. And your next actions will have consequences if you don't get them chips up. You got a week, or would you like for me to just deliver a body in front of your house?"

Silence.

Trigga pondered the threat and asked himself what was the chance of the assailant on the phone following up and making true on his threats? So far, whoever it was had been batting about one thousand and following through on every threat rendered.

Finally, Trigga'a resolve shattered into a million tiny pieces like cracked glass.

"Okay, man, give me a week. I'll come up with the money, but how do I know you ain't gon' keep fuckin' with me and my family."

"You don't know, but remember this. I am with you at all times. I can even see you right now. So please don't underestimate me or it could be you dressed out in one of them silky expensive white caskets."

"But how—"

CLICK!

Just as Trigga was about to ask how to get the money to him, the line disconnected.

Trigga continued to lie over the steering wheel with his eyes closed, mind searching for a solution to his predicament. Then all of a sudden, there was a loud bang on the window. Startled, he reached for his banger and looked up. It was a state trooper in full regalia.

"Fuck!"

4

---

a large ominous shadow loomed over him. The ardent bright sun cast a piercing light in Trigga's eyes as he glared up at the cop.

"Is everything alright?" the cop asked as he peered into the car. Even though he had on mirrored shades, Trigga could tell the cop was focused on the backpack positioned in his back seat.

"Yeah, yeah, I'm good," Trigga said as he furtively stashed the gun under his thigh.

"You parked illegally on the side of the road. You been drinking?" the cop asked in a countrified voice as he eased his head inside the car, sniffing.

"Just a family emergency. I was stressed out. I didn't want to cause an accident, so I pulled over—"

"Lemme see your license and registration," the cop said impassively and ducked his head further into the car.

"Damn!" Trigga exclaimed with a frown in contempt for the cop's aggressive behavior.

"Wha'cha got in dat dere book bag." His breath smelled of nicotine.

"Books, why?"

"License and registration," the cop barked and pulled his head out the car. Trigga hoped he didn't see the banger under his lap, or the guns in the backpack, for the matter. For the life of him, he couldn't remember if he left the bag open.

After Trigga had fished in his wallet for his I.D., he gave it to the cop.

"I hope I didn't do anything wrong. Like I was trying to say, it's a family emergency."

"Just keep your hands on the steering wheel and don't do nuttin' that might get you in trouble."

"Okay, and when my license comes back clean, I gotta go. My wife is in the hospital." Trigga was on pins and needles. New York had recently passed a gun law where a convicted felon could get life for carrying a gun.

"Yeah, yeah, sure. Everything comes back clean, you free to go," the cop said and walked off. For the first time, Trigga was filled with a sense of relief as he watched the cop walk to his patrol car from his rearview mirror. He just happened to look at the ashtray and there was a partial blunt. He scooped it up with the quickness and ate it, and the same time, he pushed the banger under his leg and took several deep breaths to calm his nerves, as he prayed like a muthafucka he didn't have any warrants from back in the day still pending.

Then to his horror, as cars with people gawking at him sped by on the expressway, several other state trooper cars pulled up with their lights flashing too, and pulled up right behind him.

"Ohh, shit!" Trigga said full of dread, as his heart beat fast in his chest like a bass drum. He continued to watch as the cops huddled in discussion, and for a nanosecond, Trigga thought about bolting from the car.

Three of the cops turned and trailed in a lane, walking towards his car. As the New York wind swirled, cars raced by. One cop in particular positioned himself on the passenger side just in case maybe Trigga tried to make a dash for it.

"Would you mind stepping out the car so we can search it?" the cop asked for the first time as he tipped his Stetson five-gallon hat with a hint of politeness.

"For what?" Trigga raised his voice and intentionally made eye contact with the rest of the cops as the sun glared in his face.

"I see you got an extensive criminal record, suspect in murders, did some time in prison—"

Trigga cut him off. "What that got to do with you asking me to search my car?"

"Just making sure you ain't got no weapons and guns."

"Okay, I'll save you the trouble. NO, I ain't got no weapons and guns, and I know my constitutional right. You can't search my car without a probable cause."

"Oh, you's a smart one," one of the cops chimed in. He was short and rotund with a huge pot belly, and cheeks were ruby red showing anger.

"No, I's just knows my rights," Trigga said, mimicking the cop. His face turned a shade redder. On the other side of his vehicle, Trigga could see another cop shield his eye from the sun as he tried his best to look inside his car.

"Boy, we not going to ask you no more! Step outside the car—"

"BOY! Fuck you calling a boy?" Trigga asked, and just that fast, the moment was becoming as volatile as the race relations in America. Just then, one of the cops, the short pot belly one un-holstered his gun.

"Now, boy, we not going to ask you again to step outside the car, or you gone be charged with obstruction of justice."

Trigga eased his hand for the gun under his seat. For some strange reason, he was more agitated than anything with little regard for his life or his liberty. The friction between white police officers and Black men was genocidal.

"I toldja, I ain't no fuckin' boy! And why in the fuck am I being harassed when I ain't done shit?"

"You was parked on the side of the road suspiciously," the cop that had pulled him over said.

"Ain't no fuckin' law called suspicion. Y'all just fuckin' with me because I'ma nigga and done shit, and I ain't getting out no fuckin' car 'cause it's my constitutional rights!" Trigga was yelling. He was so furious there were large veins protruding from his forehead as his mouth spewed spittle.

Just then, the potbelly cop flung the car door open and grabbed Trigga by his shoulder. The other cop that had been by the passenger door rushed over; he was certain there was about to be a melee.

In Trigga's blind rage, he reached under his leg for the banger, fully intent on shooting the cop in his dome and having trial on the streets. Just when the tussle was about to ensue and a violent gun battle about to erupt, there was a loud halting voice, a thick baritone, like rumbling thunder.

"What is going on here, Albert?" the cop yelled as he rushed over. He was the only cop with a white shirt. He was a mammoth of a man, at least six feet seven with broad shoulders and a large barrel chest. The label on his gold name tag read Sergeant Davenport.

The cop that had pulled Trigga over began to explain. "Serg, I pulled him over because he was suspiciously parked on the side of the road—"

"There ain't no law stating that I can't pull over to the side of the road. They just fuckin' with me. I told him I had a family emergency."

"He's lying," the cop replied.

"Did you run his tag and driver's license?" the sergeant asked as he walked up. His eyes were the bluest green that Trigga had ever seen, with his auburn colored hair and suntanned complexion.

"Hell yeah! I showed him my driver's license and everything. Now he talkin' about just because I have been in trouble with the law before I need to let him search my fuckin' car."

The sergeant's eyebrows knotted up as he turned and looked at the cop for an answer. The other two cops hesitantly stepped back, feigning innocence.

"I just merely asked could I search the car because he had been in trouble before, then he got all loud and belligerent!"

"You telling a muthfuckin' lie!" he shouted from the driver's seat.

The sergeant pressed his paper-thin lips as if in contemplation, as the wind blew at his hair. Then he stuck his head inside the car and tried to talk as polite as possible.

"Tell you what, let's just do it simple. You let my men search the car. We don't find anything and you're free to go, huh, pal?"

Trigga couldn't believe what he was hearing. They were back to square one. With ever fiber in his body, he tried his best to bridle his nerves as he spoke with his jaw clenched tight.

"Man, I keep fuckin' telling y'all, I know my fuckin' rights. You can't just pull me over for no fuckin' cause and search me or my car for no reason."

"Right, but I can ask you, and if there is reason for suspicion, I can bring in a K-9 unit to have them sniff your car for drugs."

"Man, fuck!" Trigga scoffed, and slammed his hand on the steering while causing one of the cops to jump like a gun had been fired.

"This is Sergeant Davenport. I'm on interstate 90, exit ramp 14. Can you send a K-9 unit?" the sergeant said as Trigga just looked at him in disbelief. Things were going from bad to worse.

"Are you fuckin' serious?!" Trigga asked as he looked up at the sergeant.

"It won't take but a minute and you're free to leave," the sergeant said as his blueish green eyes sparkled ominously in the sunlight.

Trigga's phone chimed. He looked at the caller and it was a blocked number. He answered it anyway just to stall for time.

"Hello, this is doctor Steven." The Bluetooth in the car speakers was loud enough for the police to hear and they all listened attentively.

"Hi, Doc, you kinda caught me at a bad time," Trigga said.

"I'm sorry, but this is important. Your wife's condition has worsened. One of her kidneys has shut down. We are concerned she is deteriorating. Her body may be going into catalepsy."

"Cat-what?" Trigga retorted baffled.

"Catalepsy is a condition of suspended animation and loss of voluntary motion in which the limbs remain in whatever position they are in because the brain cannot send signals."

"What are you sayin', Doc?" Trigga asked in a choked voice riveting with fear.

"She has not come out of the induced coma; her body is not responding."

"Ohhh, man, nooo," Trigga wailed, and hung his head on the steering wheel crestfallen, and began to bang his fist on the dashboard. Each of the cops looked at each other with empathy; they heard the conversation. The potbelly cop shot his partner a grim expression and was acknowledged with a subtle shrug.

A blue and white scripted New York police cruiser pulled up. Inside, the sound of a dog barking was echoed on the highway. Trigga looked into the rearview mirror as the K-9 Unit parked. His eyes were scarlet red like he had been crying blood tears. He looked like he had aged ten years in the last five minutes.

The sergeant stuck his head inside the car. This time his voice had a softer tone when he spoke; not as a racist cop, but as a human.

"You gotta keep it together. I lost my aunt to cancer. It's not over, she might pull through. You got any children by her?"

Trigga couldn't even look the cop in the eyes as he stared straight ahead. He was consumed with a gall of emotions, a feeling he had never experienced before.

"Yeah, I got a little boy by her," Trigga said melancholically, as he gripped the steering wheel so tight his knuckles paled. In the rearview mirror, he watched as the cop took a ferocious looking German Shepherd out the vehicle.

Suddenly, the sergeant turned to the cop that had first approached the vehicle with the traffic citation. They walked to the shoulder of the road as traffic passed like they were on a raceway.

"He's distraught; his wife is fighting for her life in the hospital. That may be the possible cause for his erratic behavior. What did he tell you when you first approached his vehicle?"

The cop adjusted his wide brim hat as a caravan of yellow school buses passed by. "He did say he was experiencing a family emergency and that his wife was in the hospital."

Just then, the dog handler approached with a huge German Shepherd.

"George, just do a quick run through for drugs," the Sergeant said to the handler.

"Sure," the handler said. He looked nerdy; he wore thick bifocal glasses, and a dirty wrinkled uniform with combat boots that looked too big for his feet.

Trigga watched as the dog sniffed at his car. In his pocket was a quarter ounce of loud, and in the ashtray, was a graveyard of burned blunt roaches.

Suddenly in his rearview mirror, Trigga saw cops dispersing one by one to their vehicles and absentmindedly, he exhaled a deep sigh of relief.

"You're free to go," the original cop said. For some reason, his demeanor had changed.

Trigga didn't trust his voice to speak, so he gave a tacit nod as a ball of sweat distilled down the side of his forehead. He was still gripping the steering wheel, looking straight ahead, devastated.

"Next time don't be so difficult; when a police officer asks you to do something, comply! You people act like you have a problem with authority."

Trigga just turned his head and looked at the cop, carved out in the bright sun, and gave him a blank expression. He had enough guns in the car to get him a couple life sentences, so rational set in over irrational.

"Yes, sir," came a terse response. The cop did a brief double take looking at Trigga, then added, "I hope your wife gets better. Have a nice day."

He walked off into the sun.

"Fuck ass crackah," Trigga growled under his breath and placed the car in gear and sped up. He had a plan. By that time, somebody was going to tell him something, or more bodies were going to start dropping by the dozens.

5

As soon as he walked into the Gentleman's Club, as much as he hated to admit, its grandiose elegance was intimidating. The ambiance was straight out of something you would expect to see in a Vegas strip club. And even the waitresses wore exotic gold sparkly two-piece outfits that left little to the imagination. The club was packed full of patrons as a song by the rapper, Future, played. The aroma of weed was heavy in the air as Trigga navigated towards the bar. It, too, was packed with people of all races and ages. But what stood out the most to him was the opulent décor. Everything was made out of shiny gold and bronze, ensconced with purple velvet on the walls and floors.

Trigga spotted a table right next to the stage. He had to do a double take as he neared. There was a fucking lion in a cage at the back of the stage, as blue, purple, and green lights strobed it. The lion paced back and forth in the cage uneasily. Directly in front, a stripper danced. She was a white girl with full body tatts and body piercings; even her crotch had a tattoo of a serpent. Her spectacular shape was curvaceous, mostly ass and tits with a small taut waist. She had flaming red hair that flowed down to her back and chatoyant eyes that held mystery. She donned six-inch stiletto heels as she acrobatically hung upside down from the stripper pole, riding the heavy bass line, then she let go and her body flung itself backwards spiraling through the air. She landed on her hands and did a backwards flip, and came down on her feet and did a split then bounced with it, scrubbing her pussy against the floor. The patrons began to make it rain, throwing money on stage. Trigga had never seen anything like it before. The stripper was standing damn near knee deep in paper money, and most of the money he noticed was from dope boys and affluent, wealthy white men.

APPLAUSE!

Even the fuckin' lion growled, and despite Trigga's ill temperament, he was spellbound, so he had to applaud. It suddenly dawned on him as he looked around, why his club was losing money; the entertainment was incredible! He spotted a couple of ex stripper, coke heads, Genia and Diamond; they were some of his best money makers. It also dawned on him as soon as he saw them why they left. It was business, he shouldn't take it personal. But he did. He felt more than a pang of jealousy. He felt envy. White folks with money were taking over the strip club business. And where in the fuck did they get a lion from?

"Baby, would you like to smoke a hookah and a take a shot to kick off your evening in the Gentleman's Club? My name is Passion," an attractive waitress said in a cute sing-song voice. She was drop dead gorgeous with a shapely figure, long pretty legs, and her dark-chocolate mahogany skin seemed to glow under the radiant lights. But what got him was her smile. She had perfect white teeth and dimples. Her hazel eyes dazzled him, as she stood so close the fragrance of her perfume enticed his nostrils. For some reason, he found himself staring at her midriff, her navel ring, and the sheer silk material beneath it. She wasn't wearing any panties, and it was obvious her pussy was shaved bald.

"Uh, yeah, can I got a shot of Hennessy and Coke on the rocks," Trigga said and pulled his eyes away from her and reached in his pocket and passed her a crisp hundred-dollar bill.

"Would you like a hookah?" She pushed up on him, only inches from his face, and it was tempting like pussy on a platter, but Trigga was a discipline.

"Naw'll, I'm good, ma." He waved her off and stole a glance as she sashayed away with ass for days.

"Next on the stage, it's your favorite bad bitch, Goddess," the deejay said, and the crowd erupted with boisterous applause. The music changed to a Kanye West song and the lights dimmed then came back on. The stage scenery had changed. Some type of heavy thick fog permeated and the floodlights turned pink and red, flashing, and out of the fog, there was a huge pink king-size bed and some thick chick lying on her back, gyrating, humping the air, legs spread wide with pink pussy galore. Trigga sat straight up in his seat as a bellow of dense fog evaporated, raising to the ceiling. He continued to stare. The stripper had blond hair and high cheekbones with slanted eyes that looked familiar.

"Here is your drink. Are you sure you don't want to try some hookah? It's only thirty dollars," the waitress asked and pushed up closer in his face with an attempt to block his view. Her fragrance was still enticing.

"Naw'll, I'm good, shawtie. Who dat stripper is up there?" Trigga asked and ducked his head to get a better look at the stripper in bed, ignoring the commotion coming from the other side of the club. He recognized the John Doe Boys. They were gangstaz and drug lords. They had garbage bags full of money, making it rain. They used to frequent his club; now he knew why they stopped coming months ago.

The waitress intentionally blocked his view again, placing her torso only inches from his face when she bent down eye level to make sure he got a full view of her magnificent breasts, confined in the chic transparent material.

"That's Goddess. If you want her, I can get her for $2,500, then there is me." She stood all the way up and danced, doing a 360, shaking her ass and breasts in his face. "I would love to spend some quality time with you for $1,500. I'm younger, more tighter, wetter; I'll be twenty-one next June," she purred in a breathy timbre in his ear; succulent lips and tongue caressed his earlobes as she rested her hands on his thigh and stroked it seductively. Instantly, Trigga felt a hard-on coming. This was the allure of the strip club; pussy entrapment... more poisonous than a deadly cobra, with venom just as potent to an unsuspecting victim.

Trigga pulled himself away and ducked his head around the waitress and looked back on stage as a few dollar bills sailed by him. Again, he found himself staring...

"Well, dayum!" The waitress suddenly had an attitude. "If you like that old bitch on stage that much, I told you, for the money, I can get her for you."

Trigga could barely hear a word she said as he stared, mystified at the stage, then it hit him!

"Muthufucka-goddamnit-sonofabitch. That's fuckin' Red. The bitch that set me up!" he said under his breath with his mind racing a mile a minute.

"Uhh, ex-cuse YOU! Did you just say something?" the waitress asked, suddenly. Her once polished demeanor was ghettofied as she stood with hands on her wide hips, succulent lips pushed to the side of her face.

Trigga quickly regained his composure with a plan quickly formulating in his mind. "I said muthufuckin-goddman-right. I wanna trick with both of y'all."

"Trick?" She bobbed her head and frowned at him like he had just violated one of the most protected cardinal rules of a stripper. It's never called selling pussy or trickin'. The correct term is sponsor. Trigga quickly corrected his blunder. "I wanna sponsor both y'all."

"Humph, you sure your money right?" the waitress asked above the roar of the music and laughter. Someone on the other side of the club was trying to get her attention; she threw up a finger. "One minute, baby."

Trigga reached into his pocket and removed a wad of cash; about ten stacks that made her eyes bulge with greed. "Bitch, if I tell you a duck can pull a truck, you better hook 'em up. Not only do I have enough cash to pay you, but I'm giving tips on some big boy shit!" he bragged, and peeled off 3 one-hundred-dollar bills.

The waitress couldn't help but laugh out loud. Not only was he handsome as fuck, but he was funny and caked up with lots of dough.

Trigga pulled her close. "Dig, shawtie. A nigga ain't tryna grandstand on front street, na'mean? I'm on some low-profile shit, you dig. So here is what I want you to do. After her set, y'all meet a nigga in the parking lot. I got some coke and some molly, and I'm smoking on some bomb ass loud. We can go back to my place and chill, feel me."

She eased in closer with her brow in a tight line across her forehead. "But I don't get off 'til two in the morning," she complained. Trigga peeled off five more hundred-dollar bills. "Bitch, make it happen and a nigga still gon' break you off with the fifteen hundred and a tip. I toldja I'm on some big boy shit," Trigga said, and leaned all the way back in his seat and grabbed his dick for emphasis.

All she could do was blush at his antics; plus, the fact he was thugged out and bold with it, and the large dick print in his pants didn't hurt either. That really turned her on. She eased closer between his legs, so close that he could feel the heat from her body when she said, "Nigga, you ain't gotta tell me twice, me and Goddess will meet you in the parking lot." With giddiness, she abruptly turned and wiggled her ass as she walked off just as some irate customer approached. She ignored him and headed straight for the back of the stage. Trigga watched with his heart beating fast in his chest. He needed for Red to take the bait. His intent was to lure them to a secure spot and beat Red's ass, possibly even torture her if need be, until she told him what he needed to know. He wanted to know who was the nigga that set up his place to be robbed, killed his O.G. homie, J.B., kidnapped his son, and brutally beat his wife nearly to death.

Just then, Trigga looked up as the stripper, Diamond, that used to work for him took the stage. He just so happened to notice Passion, the waitress that he had sent to get Red. She was standing by the stage with Red, pointing in his direction. Trigga abruptly turned and ducked his head in a nick of time, with his back towards them. He bounced towards the exit. He couldn't help but notice the club had a perfect combination of hooliganism, hoes, hustlers, and dope boys, commingling with some of the white affluent patrons, sprinkled in for good measure.

A few heads turned in passing and he acknowledged some of the dope boys. Even though he was kind of in his feelings for losing what he thought were loyal customers, he understood it was the lifestyle; big booty bitches, dope money, expensive drinks and more, all in the fast lane of get rich or die trying, literally.

Out of the blue, he heard somebody calling his name. He looked up and it was Gina. She was a dancer that used to work at his club. She sold more pussy than a little bit, and snorted coke like it was candy.

"Shit!" He cursed under his breath and abruptly stopped in his tracks. The last thing he wanted was for Gina to alert Red of his presence because he knew, without a shadow of a doubt, she would get ghost again and run like a rabbit.

At that exact moment, unbeknownst to Trigga, he was headed straight for danger. At a table right in front of him, next to the bar, was Austin, with a fitted cap pulled down over his head, and sitting directly across from him was Lania. She just happened to look up and see Trigga headed straight for them. A shiver of pee squirted in her panties.

Her worse nightmare was about to be confirmed. Trigga had found out she was in cahoots with Austin and he was about to kill them both.

Things were about to get ugly and fast.

6

"Austin, don't turn around, but Trigga is coming up behind you!" Lania whispered. Her voice was full of fear as she ducked her head and placed her hand over her face. Fortunately for her, Trigga had his focus on something else going on in the club.

"Bitch, fuck you talkin' 'bout!" Austin quipped with alarm in his thick voice and came up with his .9mm. The chrome metal plate sparkled ominously in the dim light as Austin turned all the way around in his seat anyway, after she told him not to. There was no way he was going to let Trigga get the ups on him, especially after all the diabolical shit he had done to him. Austin's intent was to kill him immediately.

As fate would have it, when Austin turned around to start blasting, Trigga wasn't paying him the slightest attention. He was being accompanied by some gorgeous nude stripper chick with a phat ass and a pretty face. Both her nipples were pierced with gold loops. Trigga appeared not to be paying him any attention at all; in fact, he was heavy into the conversation, but still, Austin watched intensively as if his very life depended on it, and it did. With Trigga's back turned, Austin ducked down in his seat and placed his banger on his lap. Luckily, the club was dimly lit and no one saw his actions.

Then something sinister occurred to him and it didn't help matters more that he was high as fuck off coke.

"Bitch, fuck wrong witcha?! What, you tryna set a nigga up? What the fuck this nigga doing here?" he asked, and reached for Lania, grabbing her by her throat. She pulled away and scratched at his hand, drawing blood.

"Hell naw'll, and don't be puttin' yo'- fuckin'-dick beaters on me. We ain't at home, nigga, we in public!" she snapped with her lips tight across her teeth as she reared back like a feline cat about to strike. Austin looked between her and her drink, a tall glass of dark brown liquor, and it dawned on him, *this bitch faded.* He started to punch her in her shit like a man, but instead, he leaned forward, never taking his eyes off Trigga, and hissed between clenched teeth.

"Bitch, on err'thang I love, I feel like you set this shit up for Trigga to be here, or at least had something to do with it. I'll drop your ass right here with one punch. Now get your fuck ass back there and get Red. We need to get her the fuck outta here before Trigga gets on to her too, and if that happens, it's a wrap. That bitch knows everything, even where we live at."

"But..." Lania was about to say, when Austin cut her off.

"But my ass, bitch. Just do what the fuck I say. Here!" He reached into his jacket pocket and passed her a small .22 caliber pistol. In the hood, it was known as a 'throw away.' He carried it for such occasions.

She cowered, looking at the small weapon like it was a poisonous tarantula spider. "What am I supposed to do with this?" she asked terrified.

"Shoot that hoe in her dome if you can't get her in the car. This is crucial because if you don't and that nigga finds his way to her, he gone kill you and our entire plan is down the drain; all this work for nothing."

"But I thought you told me our plan was to spend some time with him and pick his brain," she said, petrified. She was hoping just to spend some more time with Trigga, since he was more vulnerable than ever because he was distraught over his wife being in the hospital, and the club was in disarray, thanks to her conniving ass.

"Bitch, you not listening to me; drinking too many of them goddamn Tequilas. The nigga about to break and give us that money, but not if this bitch blow our cover. We need to keep the pressure on him. You need to get on your job."

"It wouldn't be if you hadn't wanted to do that damn threesome. You wanna fuck everything that move," she responded emboldened. He made a mental note never to allow her to drink again when they were out plotting. She had too many drinks in her.

"I don't wanna do it. I ain't never shot a gun before," she pleaded.

"Bitch, I'ma give you an ultimatum. Either you shoot that bitch in the head, out in the parking lot, or I'ma shoot you right here, so help me gawd.

"What about my babies, and what kinda getaway plan is that? And why can't you shoot her, why meee?" Lania drawled out, drunk.

"That is the plan. Now, GO. I'll meet you in the parking lot, and if I see any funny shit between you and that nigga, Trigga, I'm just gon' walk over there and start blasting.

"What about my babies?" Lania whined.

"They will be okay. Besides, I don't think one of them mines anyway; that little red muthafucka," Austin blurted out truthfully.

"I told you to stop sayin' that." She turned the gun on him.

"Bitch, don't point dat shit at me!" he said and shoved her hand with the gun in the opposite direction.

"Man, let's go! Shoot the bitch in her dome and keep it moving. Go!"

"Don't sound like no fucking plan to me," she mumbled under her breath.

He placed the gun in her purse and shoved her so hard, she nearly fell out her seat, knocking over her drink, and causing alcohol to spill on her new Prada skirt.

"Ugh, I can't fuckin' stand your ass—"

She abruptly stopped talking; Trigga was headed in their direction. She ducked behind a booth that a couple was sitting in and headed towards the back of the stage in search of the stripper, Red.

Trigga walked right past Austin, not even paying him the slightest attention as he headed for the exit to wait for Red and Passion in the parking lot.

Trigga stood not too far from the main entrance. Two burly bouncers stood outside the club smoking cigarettes as the valets parked cars. Trigga's ears rang from the pulsating bass from the music in the club. The night air was humid as a cool breeze seemed to tingle his damp skin, bringing him back to his senses. The overhead in the sky was a full moon, embellished by a constellation of bright stars that looked like holes had been poked into the canvas of the night.

Trigga was careful to conceal himself behind a Porsche truck so that if

Red saw him before he could get to her, she didn't panic and try to escape. He needed to get her into his car.

It didn't take long. Soon, a couple of dudes walked out, followed by Red and Passion. The guys were trying to get their attention.

"Yo, with all that ass, let a nigga holla at'cha?"

"Sheit, a bitch tryna eat. No money, no honey," Passion commented followed by a ripple of laughter that came from the bouncers.

Trigga quickly turned his head and took out his phone and pretended to be in deep conversation, when he heard Passion say, "See, bitch, I told you I wasn't lying. There he go over their standing next to the truck." They both giggled girlishly and lassoed their arms around each other, then walked across the parking lot towards him, while his back was slightly turned. The echo of high heels striking across the concrete was followed by salacious catcalls.

Just as they neared, Trigga turned around. He was in arm's length, close enough to touch each of them.

"What's up?" Trigga announced with a grin.

"Wha-da-fuck?!" Red said with a scowl and took a timid step back as if she was thinking about making a run for it.

Trigga knew he needed to appease her in order to rock her to sleep and catch her off guard. Acting wasn't his best forte, but he could have been nominated for an Oscar the way he played his role.

"Dayum, Red, I didn't know that was you on stage with your fine, short ass. I apologize for what happened the last night you was at the club and some fuck niggaz tried me, but I'm good and I still got your night's pay."

"Uhh?" She gawked at him and looked around like it was some type of setup. Red was a street chick, game tight; it was going to be hard to get her to go for the okie doke.

Trigga continued, "Yeah, I'm good now. I'm just happy you're okay. When we didn't hear anything from you and you just disappeared, I thought them niggaz had got you too."

"Whaat?" She drawled with her eyebrows, a tight line across her face, like she was trying to digest everything he was saying.

"Yeah, I thought you was fucked up. I'm glad you're safe, and damn, you looking good," he said and reached out and hugged her. She didn't reciprocate and stood as still as a mannequin.

"Hold up, y'all know each other?" Passion asked quizzically with her hand on her hip.

"You fuckin' right! This a money getting bitch. My club ain't been the same since she left," Trigga exclaimed joviality.

"Club? You own a club?" Passion asked with her mouth open. Trigga was really starting to look like that nigga.

For the first time, Red spoke. "Yep, he owns a strip club, got a wife, and a baby," Red said as she held him with an icy glare. Her suspicions of him were palpable.

"Wife?" Passion frowned.

Trigga ignored Passion and kept his attention on Red. This was about to be a lot harder than he first anticipated. He had his pistol in his spine and was prepared to abduct her from the parking lot. There was only one major problem: the bouncers standing several yards away. They were there to protect the premises.

"Why? Damn, you act like you ain't happy to see a nigga. I'll keep my muthufuckin' money I owed you. I was tryna keep it one hunnid witcha'," Trigga said taking a gamble, and turned like he was about to walk away.

"Hold up, nigga!" Red ran up and grabbed his arm. "Nigga, you gon' just take a bitch money?" She smiled generically and took his hand with both of hers. Anyone watching would have thought they were old friends.

"Shit, you actin' funny style like you don't fuck with a nigga. I told you I thought you was dead or some shit, only to find out you da Goddess. And look like you done bought some tits and ass," he said with a southern twang that made Red blush for real that time. The truth was, Red had some work done on her body and was proud he noticed like the rest of the men had.

"He got a fuckin' baby and a wife and you own a strip club?" Passion pondered.

"Yeah, and my wife in the hospital in serious condition," Trigga added soberly.

"Yeah, I heard about what happened to your wife. I never really liked her, but I don't wish bad on no one. I hope she gets better," Red said, while still holding his hand.

"Well no wonder then; you probably horny as hell and you can't fuck them bitches at your club. It's like the dope game rule, you can't get high off your own supply," Passion cajoled and eased up close on him. Trigga was looking like Captain Save-A-Hoe.

"Yeah, I changed my dancing name and kept it moving after that shit happened. It was time for a serious change. I was scared, you know what I mean, baby," Red said.

"I understand. I'm just happy you good, with your fine ass, and you be killing dat shit on stage," Trigga complimented her. Red couldn't help but blush like a schoolgirl on her first date.

"I just didn't know you fuck with dancers. You was acting like you wasn't feeling none of us at the club, acting all mean and shit."

"I'm a nigga. I like to get my dick wet just like the next nigga, but like shawtie basically just said, you don't fuck bitches in your camp, dat shit bad for business. Plus, hoes talk too much."

"Huh, 'scuse you. Niggaz talk more than bitches these days. Y'all be lying on your dicks n'shit, sayin' you fucked a bitch and ain't got nowhere near the pussy," Passion sassed.

"Fo-real, girrrl!" Red added, and the two of them gave each other high fives all animated, with titties and ass jiggling. Trigga looked on. His mind was plotting on how to get rid of Passion and scoop Red up solo. Then it hit him, the perfect idea. He had some knock out drops in his stash. He would just give Passion some in her drink. Once she was out cold, he would make Red tell him what he needed to know then murk her and dispose her body, and by the time Passion woke up, he'd just tell her she left and he didn't know where she had gone.

"Okay, let's bounce. Like I said, I got some coke and Molly with some bomb ass weed. We can lace it if you like." Trigga tried to lay the deadly trap.

"Hell yeah," they both said in unison. "And don't forget that money, nigga. Total, it should be about close to five bands with your good tipping, fine ass," Passion joked as they turned to walk off towards Trigga's whip.

"Bitch, I got enough money to make it not rain, but thunderstorm in my bedroom," Trigga bragged and pulled out a knot, flashing it.

That's when he heard a female call his name. He looked up to see who it was, and to his dismay, it was Lania.

Fuck she doing here?

7

*L*ania walked up looking disheveled and drunk, as she slightly staggered. Her blouse was partially open, showing off her cleavage all the way to the nipple. There was some sort of dark stain on her dress.

"Heyyy, y'all," she called out with a crooked smile, waving her hand.

"What are you doing here?" Trigga asked since she was supposed to be back at his club, running it.

"I just happened to come through to check out all the competition. Besides, I had heard Red was working here, so I had to see for myself." Lania made up a quick lie and Trigga wasn't really buying it.

"So who is running the club then?" he asked.

"Yadi and Tory. And no need to worry, I gathered all the night's receipts before I left. Besides, there were hardly any customers in there anyway. So what y'all up to?" she asked as she strolled closer.

"We finna go back to his crib and turn up and party. Three is company and four is a crowd," Passion said rudely with a stank expression on her face.

Lania cut her eyes at the young girl, giving her a repugnant stare until Red came to her rescue.

"Unt uh, that's my bitch right there. She can come too," Red cut in.

"So I see you got other priorities nowadays, Trigga," Lania said with an attitude. She was jealous because Trigga was about to trick with them and in her heart, just as Austin had said, she had a crush on him and she wanted him all to herself. But most importantly, she was puzzled as to how she was going to get Red out the picture before she started running her big ass mouth. Then she had a bright idea. It was devious as hell, but she just prayed it would work.

She leaned back on her heels and spoke. "You're right tho', sweetheart; three is company and four is a crowd, so how about you just move it along," she said to Passion as she walked up in her face. Instantly, there was tension in the air.

"Hell naw'll! Who dis old bitch think she is, just gone stroll her ass up here calling shots," Passion retorted, looking up at Lania who had her by about three inches and twenty pounds.

"I'm finna be the old bitch that get on your ass if you keep runnin' your mouth, bum bitch!"

Lania reached back to slap her, and Trigga stepped in between them. This was not what he had expected. Things were quickly getting out of hand on some hood rat drama type shit.

"Y'all fuckin' chill!" he shouted as he pushed them apart. Several club patrons gawked at them as they passed by.

"Red, you better tell this bitch who da fuck I am before I break my foot off in her young ass!" Lania shouted to Red, but Trigga peeped the move when he saw Lania wink her eye on the sly at Red, and that was all it took. And to his surprise, Red walked into the fray, and with a deep sigh, she said, "Honey, go back inside the club. I don't think it's best you roll with us, and your mouth doin' the most right now."

Passion jerked her neck like she had been slapped. She snapped, "Bitch, I was the one set this up. I went and got your old ass to get some money, now you gon' try me like this, old triflin' ass bitch!"

"Old, triflin', and?!" Red repeated bug-eyed as her face paled with anger. "First off, thirty-five ain't old, BITCH, and who you calling trifling? At least I got ass and tits, skinny BITCH. And I'll mop your young ass up and down this parking lot, keep talking!"

"You ain't gon' do—"

Before Passion could get the words out her mouth, Red swung, hitting her in the jaw, then reached for her hair and yanked her to the ground. They fell hard, with Red landing on top of her, pummeling her with blows. The scene was pathetic, and just when Trigga reached down to pull her off, to his dismay, Lania rushed over and began to stomp the poor girl in her face, causing her head to violently hit the concrete.

"Fuck, man! Y'all fuckin' stop it!" Trigga shouted, shoving Lania so hard she fell on her ass. Just then, the bouncers that were standing in front of the club rushed over. By then, it was pure pandemonium. There was hair weave, high heels, and knock off purses littering the parking lot, as throngs of people began to stand around watching. A few of them cheered them on, others instigated.

"Damn, that bitch getting her ass whipped and she ain't got no panties on, pussy everywhere," someone chanted.

The bouncers were able to pull Red off of Passion, and to everybody's surprise, Passion got back up on her feet wearing one shoe. Her face looked like she had been attacked by a thousand angry yellow jackets.

"Damnnnn," the crowd of onlookers droned at the horrific sight of her face as blood spewed from her mouth and nose.

"Bitch, you ain't did shit." She staggered with one shoe on, punch drunk, dance walking in a circle.

From a distance in the bay of the parking lot, Austin watched and wondered what the fuck drunk ass Lania was up to, making such a fucking scene when she should have been trying to shoot Red, or at least getting Trigga away from Red. Instead, there she was, making a big ass scene so everyone could see her face. "Dumb bitch!"

Then he heard the blaring sounds of a siren approaching. The cops were coming.

As soon as Trigga heard the sirens, he quickly rushed over and grabbed Red by her elbow and shoved her across the parking lot with Lania following.

As Austin watched, for the first time, he was in fear of his life and resisted the urge to rush over and just shoot Red, killing her. That would not only be suicide, but it would be crazy. However, the reality was, if Trigga found out he was behind all the brutality, heartache, and murder, there was no doubt that Trigga would go on a Kwacha mission to kill him. So all he could do was watch in vain as Red hopped in the front next to Trigga, while drunk ass Lania got in the back, just as an ambulance pulled up in the parking lot.

Instantly, he was filled with seething rage like he had never experienced before.

I'ma kill that bitch and that fuck nigga... think a nigga stupid, I know she fuckin' him. The bitch probably tried to set me up and the shit went wrong. The nigga was supposed to have seen me here and killed me. I have a plan for her fuck ass and that ugly ass red boy of hers too, Austin thought to himself as he plotted revenge.

As soon as Trigga's BMW pulled out the parking lot, Austin followed. The coke was telling him to kill everything that moved, and indeed, that was what he intended to do. In the back seat, wrapped in a blanket was a rocket, his AK-47, with a hundred-round drum. He was going to make that bitch sing!

"Yo, what the fuck is wrong with y'all buggin' out and shit?" Trigga said just as they pulled on the road and a caravan of cop cars sped by with their lights flashing.

"Dat bitch shouldn't have tried me like that," Red raved as she adjusted her hair and makeup in the mirror. She then removed a vial of cocaine, wrapped inside a little see-thru plastic baggy, and dipped her long finger-nail inside and took a couple toots. Trigga was about to complain but thought better of it. The bitch was a coke head and that was the reality of it. *I need to use that to my advantage,* he thought as he looked in the rearview mirror at Lania. She was all stone faced like she had something on her mind.

Trigga turned up the volume on his stereo system, bumping a new Rick Ross track. Just then, Lania sat up in her seat behind him, all in his ear.

"So, we headed back to your place to chill, huh?" She had a sour expression on her face and he could smell alcohol on her breath. She continued, "I didn't know you was into ménage trois?"

Her voice lisp with a hint of sarcasm as she stared at Trigga's eyes in the rearview mirror. She thought she detected something sinister. Red took another hit of the coke and leaned her head all the way back to get more of the euphoric high before asking, "Where we going, daddy?" With her free hand, she reached over and began to caress Trigga's dick through his pants. He turned and rewarded her with a smile that looked as plastic as the fake fruit on grandma's dining room table.

"I got a room at Best Western and an ounce of coke, plus ten thousand dollars to offer you just in case you might remember anything or know anything about what happened that night we got robbed and J.B. was murked," Trigga said nonchalantly, with his eyes straight ahead. He had hit her with his gambit, a lure to get her to talk.

A death trap.

"Oh-my-fuckin-gawd!" Lania muttered under her breath. Her heart began to beat so fast in her chest, it felt like she was about to have a heart attack. Trigga was offering nearly ten times the amount that her and Austin had offered her and she knew for a fact Red was a coke whore; she would sell her mama for that amount

"Well dayum, that's a lot!" Red responded dreamy eyed as she imagined how much coke and how many outfits she could buy to work the stage. Instantly, her hand moved faster caressing Trigga. She tried her best to unzip his zipper.

"Take that bitch out. I'll suck on that motherfucker right now in the car as we drive," Red teased, but was dead ass serious.

"Bitch, pah-lease!" Lania muttered under her breath.

Trigga's zipper was stuck and wouldn't open, and Red's hands were starting to get annoying. He removed her hands and said, "Wait until we got to the room. You can get all this dick just how you like it; ten inches long and thick as a coke can." He smiled but his eyes didn't, and that gave cause for concern.

Lania's phone chimed with a text. At first she thought it was from Austin, so she checked it. It was from her silent partner, the one person that was going to help her escape her misery of being with that maniac, Austin. Yes, she loved him and even the beatings because that was his way of showing that he loved her but the cheating, and belittling her, which was the deal breaker. She had a way out. There was no cross like the double cross, so she played naive and went with it but that was only until she got what she wanted; the money.

The text read: *What is the hold up, what is taking you so long?*

She responded: *Things are not going as planned... Let me hit you back later...*

Lania had to abruptly cut her text short when she saw Red roll her eyes at her mischievously and then lean forward to attempt to whisper in Trigga's ear.

"What y'all got going on up there?" she said in a heightened tone, mostly motivated by fear. Red was about to snitch on her with the quickness, she could feel it in her gut. That was one of the hazards of fuckin' with a drug addicted thot bitch. Loyalty had a price: an ounce of coke and ten stacks, and maybe some pills for good measure.

"Oh, we ain't doing nothing. I was just about to complain. He made me stop stroking that big ole dick. Gurl, this nigga dick damn near down to his knee," Red tried to joke, but the words came out in a nervous twang as her eyes darted around the car. She was high off the coke.

Just then, Lania got another text. She knew who it was before she even read it.

Bitch, what the fuck you doing leaving with that nigga? What, you playing me now? I told you to put a bullet in that bitch skull and leave.

Her hands were shaking so bad she could hardly read the text, and what made matters worse, she caught Red stealing another glance at her in the back seat. That time, they locked eyes for what felt like eternity, and Red pulled her eyes away and glanced over at Trigga and commented dreamily out of the blue, "Ten thousand dollars and a whole ounce... The most a bitch ever had at one time was about a quarter of an ounce, and that shit had been stepped on so many times it made my nose bleed." She laughed in a nervous cackle, like a two pack a day smoker.

"I'll give you more than that if you got some good information."

"What?" Red drawled and mopped at her nose with the back of her hand like a junkie about to get a fix.

"Yeah. My wife in the hospital; somebody beat her to near death. The doctor said she may not make it. And my son was kidnapped. I was able to get him back, but—"

"Your baby was kidnapped?" Red said appalled and made a disgusting face at Lania. That sent a seismic shiver down her spine. Then Red fired up a Newport and blew a large cloud of smoke at the windshield and then turned all the way around in her seat to face Lania. "See, I ain't know that. Y'all didn't tell me dat shit, that a baby was going to be involved and his wife was going to get beat up."

"Whaat?" Trigga hadn't caught on fully because he was driving and his mind was distant thinking about Keisha and his next move.

However, Lania did, and she placed a finger over her lips attempting to silence Red who suddenly had diarrhea at the mouth. Horrified, she knew that Red's bold statements were a prologue to snitching. Red was setting the stage for her to portray herself as the innocent victim.

"What you talking about?" Trigga asked as he pulled up into the Best Western on 95th Street. It was located in the hub of the ghetto. Standing out front were a few prostitutes, crackheads, and a few stragglers.

Trigga continued to stare at Red with a quizzical expression, like he was anxiously waiting for an answer.

Lania piped in, "This bitch high as fuck off coke and ready to fuck."

Lania was trying to get them off the subject as she hit Red with a stern face, something that conveyed, "Shut the fuck up!"

"Huh, hmm, I got something to tell you," Red said, nodding her head emphatically at Trigga.

"What is it?" Trigga asked with his jaw slack with anticipation of what she was about to say.

Suddenly, the stark reality of what was about to happened occurred to Lania. If Red ran her mouth and snitched, the car they were sitting in would be Lania's casket; Trigga wouldn't hesitate to murder her. Suddenly, Lania's high wore off and she was sober as the day she was born.

"I'm sorry, Lania, but I gotta—"

Just then, there was a loud piercing knock at the car window, causing Trigga to flinch uncontrollably and reach for his burner. They all looked up to see some lady with a rag wrapped around her head. She was severely snaggletooth, missing a few teeth, and the ones she had were rotten. She wore what looked like a gray mangy t-shirt that probably once used to be white, and some cutoff jeans.

"You got a lighter?" she asked, fogging up the car window with her fetid breath.

"Hell naw'll I ain't got no fuckin' lighter!" Trigga snapped.

"What about two dollars so I can get something to eat?" the woman asked and began to scratch her neck and private area like she was infested with something that was biting her intensely.

"Man, I ain't got nothin'," Trigga responded agitated. It was obvious the woman was a crackhead.

"I'll wash your windows."

"Fuck I just said? NO!"

Trigga opened the door with so much force he nearly caused the woman to have a stroke. "Get away from my car!" he shouted at her, and then said over his shoulder to Red, "When we get in the room, you can finish telling me."

She averted her eyes at Lania and responded timidly, "Okay."

Lania's legs felt like rubber as she stepped out the car. Even her stomach started to churn, rumbling with one of them huge shit cramps people often get when they're terrified, scared to death. She did everything in her power to establish eye contact with Red, as they walked across the parking lot, headed to the room, and perhaps her last living destination. Red continued to ignore her as she walked ahead, and Lania knew she was doomed. She actually thought about taking off running because she knew once she entered that room, it would be over.

Then she remembered something: the .22 pistol that Austin had given her was in her purse. She had an idea; it was risky as fuck, but maybe it would work. She didn't really have a choice; either that or get killed. And for the first time that night, she thought about her small children and wondered would she see them again. She also thought about the daunting fact that she was terrified of guns. She has never used one before.

Perhaps she would now?

8

―――――――

The hotel room was small and dingy with a malodorous, stale stench of cigarettes, mothballs, and old mildewed furniture permeated. The wooden nightstand was stained with cigarette butt burns. As soon as Trigga closed the door, he turned to take off his jacket and looked directly at Red. So did Lania, only with a plaintive plea on her face for her not to snitch.

Red huffed repugnantly loud as she pushed her lips up to the side of her face and folded her arms over her breasts with hubris. Trigga suddenly said as if sensing something, "Well damn, y'all just gon' stand around?!"

"I'm tryna get some of dat coke and dat big ole dick of yours, nigga," Red replied jovially, and began to remove her clothes, staggering slightly as she kicked off her high heels. She reached for Trigga's zipper and he batted her hand down.

"Chill, ma. Damn, don't you got something to tell me?"

"Well damn, let a bitch get something. Let's party and get lit and fuck up some shit, and a bitch wanna deep throat dat dick." She staggered some more and pushed up on Trigga, trying to grab his dick again. He tried to smile, but it was clear that he was running out of patience, putting on an act, as he knocked her hand down again and reached into his pocket. He threw her a bag of Molly on the table and a few grams of coke. That was all Red needed to see. Then he looked over at Lania.

"Lemme holla at you for a sec?" His voice was stern. He had something on his face that was hard for Lania to discern as a quaver seized her body, causing her to hesitate and stutter step as she clutched her purse with the gun inside. At first, she thought her greatest fear had been confirmed. *He knows; this nigga is about to kill me*, she thought.

"Where y'all goin'?" Red asked as she licked her lips greedily and pulled up a chair and began to open the plastic bag with the Molly inside.

"We gotta get some extra shit out the car. I left the ounce of coke in the stash and Lania can bring back the Hennessy and Patrón. I gotta drink when I'm getting high off all these fuckin' drugs, na'mean?" Trigga grinned.

Red's demeanor changed with a tilt of her head as she stuck her entire nose in the bag with the Molly. "Okay. Y'all don't be gone all fuckin' day," she said with white powder all over her nose.

"Yeah, right!" Trigga said as he looked at her. She was disgusting. He then pulled Lania out the door when he departed. Red wasn't paying them the slightest of interest, as she poured a line of Molly on the table next to the coke and snorted.

"What da-fuck you doin' just poppin' up at the club like this? Then you do that stupid shit and jump on that girl? Somethin' ain't fuckin' right!" Trigga barked with grit in his voice, and slammed his fist into the palm of his hand for emphasis! He was irate, angry as hell, talking a mile a minute.

They were standing outside in the corridor next to an ice machine that was dripping water all over the concrete floor. The entire time, Lania had her hand in her purse. The .22 was leveled at his stomach; she had been expecting Trigga to do something foul to her. Yes, she was scared—scared enough to pull the trigger. She needed to make it back home to her children.

"I—"

He cut her off and snatched her by her arm so hard her entire body whiplashed. "This bitch help set up the robbers at the club and she also has to know who was behind having my wife beat. She gon' tell me something! I want you to catch an Uber outta this bitch, 'cause I'm finna make her tell me something and what I'm about to do ain't gon' be nice."

Lania's heart sledge hammered in her chest. She knew this was the utmost emergency. He wouldn't have to lay one finger on Red; as soon as he asked, she would tell everything, and that would be it for her and Austin, and possibly her little getaway plan.

"No, I am in this with you. I have come this far. Th...th...there is no turning back now." Her entire body trembled badly as she stumbled over her words. She was certain he had noticed it, and he had. His eyebrows pushed up like he was seeing something about her for the first time. She knew she had to do something and fast, so she pushed up close on him with her chest against his. When all else fails, there was her sex. She gave him one of her flirtatious fuck faces. Dudes were a sucker for that; except Trigga. He grabbed her arm and pulled her even closer.

"Bitch, why you shaking? Fuck you up to?" Trigga asked, looking down at her as her hair swayed in the gentle breeze.

"I...I... It's just that I'm excited. I want you to find out who did this to you and your family." She was really frightened and trying to do everything in her will to muster up the courage to stay calm. Truth be told, she didn't even like guns and had never even shot one before, but buried deep in her purse was one and she managed to hold it with her finger on the trigger.

Trigga stared at her a second too long as if he were trying to read her demeanor, then he let go of her arm. Lania exhaled a protracted sigh as her heart continued to beat ferociously in her chest. So much so it was hard for her to catch her breath. Unbeknownst to Trigga, she was seconds away from pulling the trigger, possibly shooting him in his heart.

"Okay, I'ma let you stay, but shit could get ugly fast because time is running out and Red needs to tell me something. I have a feeling she may know a lot of shit, like who is behind this and where to find them. And when I find out, I'm killin' err'thang moving!"

Lania nodded her head like a puppet as she felt her stomach knot up. That time she was sure she needed to go to the bathroom.

They entered the room and to their dismay, Red lie on the hotel bed, butt-ass naked with the TV blaring loudly. Her legs were spread wide as she feverishly stroked her pussy like it was on fire. Her eyes were glassy and bucked wide the entire time she squirmed, slithering, humping her hand.

"Dayum, what took y'all so fuckin' long?" She groaned as her fingers dug deeper in her pussy. She made some type of wanton expression like a bitch in heat.

"I got everything—" Trigga was about to say.

"I can't fuckin' tell. I don't see no drinks, and a bitch horny and thirsty as fuck. Come over here and whip out that big ole fuckin' dick, nigga, and lemme suck on it." She squirmed as her eyes momentarily got stuck in the back of her head. Her pussy was dripping wet, making some type of gushy sound, causing Trigga and Lania to exchanged dubious expressions.

With a shrug, Trigga strolled over towards the bed and pulled out a chair from under the desk and straddled it backwards. There was a large mirror where he could see Lania staring with a deadpan expression as she gnawed on her fingernails.

"I need to ask you some questions," he said evenly with a smooth voice. Lania padded closer. She was on pins and needles as Red reached out with sticky fingers, wet with her cum, and grabbed his arm. Her torso continued to grind against the bed.

"Ask me anything, but can you do it with your dick in my mouth? Damn, a bitch horny as fuck!" She stroked herself faster and moaned, making a face like she was losing her mind.

"Do you know something about the robbery, the dudes that torched the club, killed J.B., and tried to murder my wife. Like I said, I'll give you anything you want; money, sex, you already got the drugs. Tell me something, I'll give you more," Trigga tried to persuade with urgency.

"Uhh...hmmm..." Red's hand stilled on his arm as her eyes averted back and forth between him and Lania, then focused on Lania so long that Trigga cast a glance in the mirror at Lania's expression as she stood behind him. He then turned around and looked at her. Her face was pale, etched with her sheer terror. Her mouth was pulled tight, eyes wide like she was watching a horror movie.

"Wha-da-fuck!" Trigga exclaimed, sensing something was wrong. Just then, outside, there was the sound of an ambulance as the TV continued to blare. Silence stalled like tension building with each valuable second.

"Okay, I'ma tell you," Red finally said and took a big gulp of air like she was building up the courage to speak. She reached for Trigga's zipper, and he let her as she fumbled with his pants.

"Talk!" Trigga snapped with heightened anxiety.

"These bitches ain't no good. They will set you up..." As she talked, she continued to fumble with his zipper and he let her. She finally got his dick out. It was limp but still long, elongated about the length of a baby's leg.

"Damn, horse dick ass nigga," Red drawled. She was so high you could see her eyes rolling around in her head. Trigga's dick looked like a large Polish sausage in her hand, dangling as she tried to masterfully manipulate it to get it hard by stroking it.

"You want this dick and another ounce of coke? Talk and stop the fuck shit," Trigga said, opening his pants wider to give her more access.

"I just don't want to get caught up in it because this bitch help set it up," Red said as she gestured toward Lania with her forehead. The whole while trembling badly, Lania eased her hand inside her purse. She had no choice but to shoot Trigga in the back of his head as he stood with his back turned to her.

Then in the backdrop of sirens blaring, somebody was blasting music in front of the hotel from a Chevy, when a shadow crossed over in front of the window. It was moving too slow for Trigga's liking.

"Hold up, shhhh!!" He threw up a finger for silence. His hood instincts were on full alert. A shadow had passed by the window walking too slow for his liking. Then it stopped. Trigga watched it like a hulk. Then it moved past again in front of the window but stopped that time, and just when Trigga was about to reach for his banger, the door was suddenly kicked open and a barrage of shots roared like thunder. Trigga couldn't pull his strap in time and dove to the floor!

He had got caught slipping in the worst way.

9

*H*is only course of action was to dive for cover on the side of the bed right next to Red. Her body was being riddled with bullets, as large chucks of her flesh and blood covered the bed and wall like she was being struck with a chainsaw. Her head was nearly decapitated from her body by the high-powered AR-15 assault rifle as it wreaked havoc, destroying everything in its wake.

Trigga somehow managed to huddle between the bed and the wall with his feet showing. He used Red's body as a shield as the bullets continued to ravage the room, destroying it. He tried to shield himself and reach for his banger at the same as the assault rifle's blast erupted around him!

It was almost useless.

The entire time Lania was penned on the other side of the hotel door, unbeknownst to the gunman. All the gunman had to do was look over his shoulder to his left and he would have seen her wedged between the door and the wall, shivering.

Then it happened. Emboldened, the gunman took several steps forward as he continued to let loose with the assault weapon. The tumultuous sound was deafening to the ears as the wall begun to collapse by the ferocious velocity of the weapon. The room was starting to look like a demolition in progress. The entire time, Lania was a mere two feet away, within arm's reach of the gunman.

Trigga was about to be helplessly mowed down as the gunman, certain of his prey, took several bolder steps, lunging forward. The staccato of gunfire ripped through the wall, the bed, and ceiling, causing it to collapse, exposing the exterior of the bathroom as the sound continued to roar!

Trigga was a sitting duck. His leg was visible, sticking from under the bed. The gunman almost smirked at how easy a job this was to kill the so called infamous Trigga.

Piece of cake, he thought.

The entire time, all the lone gunman had to do was look behind the door and he would have spotted Lania, cowering, standing there in fear of her life. But the triggerman was so occupied with firing his weapon and killing everything that moved, especially Trigga, that he hadn't notice Lania yet. He was inches away from getting a good head shot on Trigga.

THEN SUDDENLY OUT of the blue, Trigga's arm sprung up. In its grip, was a pearl handle sixteen-shot chrome plate .9mm! The lethal weapon seemed to sparkle in ominous gloom as Trigga blindly began to return fire, his hand jerking with each shot released.

BLOCKA! BLOCKA! BLOCKA! BLOCKA!

The gunman was struck in the shoulder as one of the bullets graced Lania's face, barely missing her skull. Bullets were flying everywhere. Lania couldn't help it, that was too much to bear. Frightening her out her wits, she had a bowel movement in her panties as she screamed to the top of her lungs, startling the gunman, causing him to momentarily turn his head as he continued to fire.

And for an infinite moment in time, Lania and the gunman's eyes locked with sheer terror. Even concealed with a ski mask covering his face, Lania could tell by the red bloodshot eyes who the gunman was.

"Aus..." Lania muttered and slid down the wall as the fusillade of shots continued to ring out.

The word came out minced, jagged from somewhere in the back of her throat where terror resided. Austin staggered backwards out the door after being hit several times in the chest, causing his body to jump with each shot. He made a wheezing sound from his breath being knocked from his lungs.

After he was gone, the sulfuric smell of gunpowder, along with acid stench of blood, was heavy in the air, along with what looked like a halo of gun smoke and debris from the walls collapsing.

Trigga climbed from under the bed. His hair and face were covered with some type of lint, smeared with sweat, and his shirt was soiled red, full of crimson blood. It looked like he was severely wounded as he trudged over to the door and peered out with his gun in hand. Being a true to life gangsta, Trigga extolled.

"I got his fuck ass! Bitch ass nigga come out better tryin' the lottery. He got a better chance of winning than fuckin' wit' me!" Trigga boasted, doing everything but beating on his chest as Lania sat hunched down, shaking and crying hysterically behind the door as she looked up at Trigga, gorily covered in blood from head to toe.

"You shot him?" The words accidentally escaped her mouth. She had expressed sympathy for the gunman but she couldn't help it; she was traumatized with her hands shaking badly.

"You mufuckin' right I shot 'em! Fuck wrong wit' you?! Dat nigga someplace leaking right now 'bout to give up the ghost," Trigga said after he looked out the door. There was a line of blood all the way down to the stair exit. Lania bawled, crying harder.

Trigga shook his head at her, baffled, as he extended a bloody hand to help her up. She ignored it as she continued to cry. Trigga suddenly flinched like he had remembered something, then turned around to look at Red.

"Sheeit!" he scuffed, disappointed. Her body was so badly badgered and grotesquely disfigured, it looked like she had been attacked with a hatchet. There was a large chunk of flesh missing from her face. Her neck was barely connected to her body and blood ran like a river.

"Fuckin' bitch dead!" Trigga scoffed and kicked the bed as he walked over examining her body as if she would suddenly spring back to life.

"Ohhh, gawd, I can't take this. This is too much!" Lania wailed. She was on the brink of having a nervous breakdown. Her baby daddy was shot and possibly mortally wounded, probably dead in the gutter out on the streets, and a woman lie in bed with her brains splattered across the carpet and walls.

"Lard, pah-lease, help me," she cried, her face covered with a melancholy expression.

In the distance, a siren blared, or perhaps it was the police. Whatever it was, Trigga began to move with urgency.

"We gotta get the fuck outta here. Them folks comin' in a minute and I ain't tryna be here!" Trigga exclaimed as he rushed around the room, wiping down his prints.

"But you're shot too, you might die," Lania clamored.

"Hell naw'll, a nigga ain't shot; bitch blood on me. I'm Gucci... lucky to be alive. You might have saved my life. That fuck nigga was about to walk right over and slaughter my ass with the big ass AR-15 until he saw you behind the door. That's when I wet his ass up."

For some reason, Lania cried harder and Trigga thought she was crying because she was distraught and scared, but the real reason was because she feared she had played a factor in Austin's death. Trigga suddenly felt sympathy for her, especially for what she had done. He bent down and tried to hoist her to her feet and suddenly sniffed the air with a frown. "Fuck dat smell is?" he asked with contempt as he continued to frown at her.

Weakly, she responded with a ball of snot rolling off her tear-stained face, "I messed myself up." Trigga interjected disdainfully.

"Hell naw'll, bitch, you done shit on yourself. You gon' have to catch an Uber to the crib. You ain't finna fuck my whip up," he complained.

Just then, a crackhead peeked her head inside the room. It was the same dope fiend that approached the car begging when they first pulled up in the parking lot.

"Heyyy y'all, the popo just pulled into the hotel. They about eight cars deep—" Then she did a double take. "What the fuck? Goddamn, y'all done murdered that gurl!" the crackhead yelled.

The entire time the dope fiend spoke her, eyes roamed the room in search of something, anything to steal including the dead woman's bloody shoes, even if they were on her feet. This was the common ecology of the hood. The stripper Red was wearing some red bottom stiletto shoes and they would go missing for a quick fix of crack. Dope fiends were like hyenas in the hood. They didn't discriminate; dead or alive, they lived to take, to feed their insatiable addiction to drugs by any means necessary.

"Bitch, get the fuck outta here." Trigga peeped the junkie move and recognized game. He decided to help Lania to her feet, even though the shitty fumes coming from her ass were overbearing. He knew he needed to move fast.

"Purrahh." He huffed in disgust at her stank odor as he helped her up, and that was when he heard the shuffling of feet and saw the reflection in Lania's eyes as they spread wide with fear.

"Trigga!" she called out his name.

He suddenly turned around and it was like a scene from the walking dead. There were at least a half a dozen junkies; they had multiplied that fast. One of them had a baseball bat; the other had a butcher knife that looked rusty with old serrated edges. Another had a large wooden table leg with crude nails sticking out of it like it could do a lot of damage if used for a weapon.

"Fuck y'all want!? Fuck all y'all doing in here?" Trigga raised his voice, filled with alarm. The thing with junkies was they were unpredictable, especially with the allure of drugs and money. That was a junkies' paradise, worthy of dying for.

"Don't try'ta buck. Just give up the money and dope and you can leave outta here, Trigga." The dope fiend with the broken off table leg called Trigga by his name, and instantly the hairs on his back stood up as Trigga narrowed his eyes into tiny slants examining the formative figure's face. It was a big guy that stood about six feet eight, with a scraggly beard and large belly. Even though it was hot outside, he wore a tattered army jacket and Thoroughbred blue jeans. Trigga knew the scraggly face from somewhere.

But where?

Then suddenly it hit him and Trigga prayed he was wrong. Trigga thought he remembered the face of one of them but he wasn't sure.

"Bear... Tom Coleman?" Trigga muttered mostly to himself, accidentally calling out the man's government.

"Yeah, nigga, it's me, live up in dis bitch," Bear exclaimed in a deep, throaty voice that had a baritone cadence that felt like it made the room shift. He pointed the crude table leg at Trigga's face in a threatening manner, not hiding his menacing intent. The entire time, more junkies and a few of Bear's clique continued to fill the room with the murmur of voices droning with "ooh's" and "ahh's" in fascination of the naked dead chick.

Another day in the life in times of the ghetto.

Bear used to be a notorious jack boy back in the day that robbed only big-time dope boys, kingpins, and mostly money getting niggas. Actually, he was a hood legend. He had even touched some celebratory rappers too, and was rumored to be the trigger man behind one of the most famous rappers getting shot nine times. That rapper lived to write a hit song about it. Bear's only problem, which ultimately lead to his hood demise, was he started getting high on his own supply of coke, and that made him worse. He was a mere husk of his former impetuous self because of his addiction. The extravagant lifestyle, money, the hood fame, and chicks were gone, but he was still respected by most and feared by all, including Trigga, who had no choice but to respect the O.G.'s gangsta.

"I gotta get outta here, Bear. Them folks coming. You see what the fuck goin' on in here," Trigga said, conscious that his banger was in his back pocket, a severe blunder on his behalf, but he had placed it there when he went to bend down and help Lania up on her feet.

"Yeah, I see what's going on; you eating good, young nigga... Gone and break bread.'"

"And he got a fly ass whip." The female crackhead chimed in as she habitually began to scratch her privates then absentmindedly smelled her fingers just as three of Bear's dope fiend goons walked behind Trigga with larceny in their intent.

"Triggaaaa," Lania crooned with fear in her voice as she clutched her purse.

Time was of the essence. Trigga was trapped and needed to make a quick escape as sirens blared. But the danger was palpable, thick as smoke in a burning room. And with only one real recourse, he had no choice. It was either he risk all and go for the gun in his pants pocket, or end up getting beaten badly, robbed, possibly killed or worse, end up in prison, probably charged with two dead bodies because of some stupid ass junkies.

"So what's it going to be, young nigga? Either you can give it or I can take it, and you know how that works." Bear's raspy thick voice boomed like thunder.

Trigga counted backwards from five in his mind as he expelled a deep breath and replied, "Okay."

"Okay, what?" Bear asked in a husky voice. For some reason, he was getting jittery, all anxious, as he stepped forward, his eyes still wandering around the room, back and forth from the dead girl's to the iced-out crucifix around Trigga's neck.

"Okay, I'ma give you what you want," Trigga said and reached for his banger. Pulling it out, he aimed, pushing the barrel straight in Bear's face, and pulled the trigger. The timing was perfect, as the fear registered on Bear's face. Even he recognized he was too late as he flailed his arms as if to ward off the bullet.

Too late!

CLICK! CLICK! CLICK!

The gun was empty. Trigga had used all the bullets shooting it out with the masked assailant.

10

Trigga continued to pull the trigger even though reality had set in; he was doomed.

His life was over.

They would devour him like what they were: a pack of hood hyenas outnumbering their prey.

Trigga helplessly threw the gun at Bear, and from there, all hell broke loose!

At least seven deep, they rat-packed Trigga, jumping on him, beating him with their fists and other crude instruments as Trigga made a valiant attempt to fight back, but it was useless. Then to Lania's horror, she witnessed one of the guys draw back to stab Trigga with what looked like an ancient, rusty old butcher knife, and that was all she needed to see. With her hand nestled in her purse, gun clutched in her hand, she pulled the trigger on the small .22 handgun.

POP! POP! POP!

The sound echoed like firecrackers on the Fourth of July as several bodies dropped. Someone screamed in agonizing pain. It was the guy wielding the knife. Suddenly, there was a stampede at the door. Dope fiends that didn't want to get shot. Two more bodies lie, sprawled out on the blood-stained carpet; Bear and the guy with the knife. Only Bear was still alive. She had shot him twice; once in the back of the head and neck. His fitful breathing sounded like someone was trying to suffocate a huge animal that wasn't dying.

"Uhhhggg, uhhggg, uhhggg." Bear struggled to breath. His mighty belly rose and fell as he gasped for badly needed oxygen. His sanguine face, paled, soaked in his own blood, etched in the terror of dying.

Trigga sprang back to his feet with the quickness, only there was a knot growing atop his right eye; his lip and nose was bleeding from the superficial wounds, but he was alive.

"Let's go! Let's go! Let's go." By then, Lania was past hysterical, more like a raving lunatic on the brink of losing it all.

"Gimmme dat gun!" Trigga yelled. He was winded like his breath couldn't catch, and his eyes bore traces of a demonic man that had been pushed past the brink of no return.

Lania wiggled her head, "NO" as she looked at Trigga slightly bent over, gasping, trying to catch his breath. Then out of the blue, he snatched the gun out of her hands and staggered over to Bear. For some reason, Trigga's hand trembled when he took aim at Bear's head, close range. Bear flinched as he gurgled blood and words plaintively, "Don't shoot."

"Trigga, no! Don't kill him!" Lania shrieked fearfully.

Trigga had his back to her when he spoke forcefully, and he repeated a ghetto cardinal rule, "Never try to kill a man and don't finish the job because if you fail, he will surely come back to do you!"

POP! POP!

Trigga took aim; one to his cranium and another to his eye socket at close range. As Lania stood there watching, her legs turned to rubber and she almost passed out. Trigga had to catch her, then he sniffed the air.

"Man, you smell like shit. You gone have to ride in the trunk."

They made it out the door and down the outside corridor. Directly in front of them was a trail of blood; Austin's blood. Trigga was expecting to see a platoon of cops and some mo' shit, but that was not the case. What he did see was a bunch of junkies and hustlers watching him. There were no cops in the parking lot, but he could still hear the sirens blaring. The dope fiends must have lied, trying to incite fear in them and knock them off guard when they said the cops was all in the parking lot.

The cops were most definitely coming, just as Trigga and Lania made it to the car.

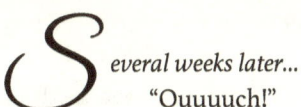 *everal weeks later...*

"Ouuuuch!"

Trigga gritted his teeth and forced himself not to run to Keisha's aid as she tried to maneuver around their home with the help of a cane. Although he wanted nothing more than to be by her side, assisting her through her recovery, he knew that he needed her to be strong. He needed her to get well and to depend on herself for the sake of herself as well as their children.

Both of their children.

By the grace of God, who still seemed to have love for a nigga like him, after several weeks of Trigga staying by her side, Keisha awoke from the coma with her life, along with the life of their unborn child. After more tests than he could count were ran, she was released to come home and recover on her own. There was one major problem: Keisha couldn't remember anything about what had happened to her or even what had occurred between them. The last thing she could recall was getting Cameron ready for his first day of school.

With the doctor constantly invading their privacy along with Trigga's determination not to stress his wife, he hadn't pressed for her to try to remember anything that she couldn't. Even though he wasn't positive he'd killed the man responsible for all of his past troubles, he hadn't heard anything from him recently therefore he allowed her time to recover at her own pace. However, there was one thing that he couldn't get out of his mind.

And now that Keisha seemed to be able to get around a little better, he figured this was the perfect time to question her about it.

"Keesh, I need you to sit down for a minute. Up here with me," he clarified, patting the chair next to him at the kitchen table.

He watched as Keisha pressed her lips together in determination, lips that were so perfect to him—lips that he'd kill a nigga over if he'd ever even thought to kiss—and positioned herself with her cane to walk over to him. She had only a slight wobble and Trigga knew that was only because of her intense level of focus. Just as much as he wanted her to get better, she wanted the same. She didn't like to feel like she was a handicap to her family.

Keisha tried to sit down in her chair with ease, but her knees buckled and she flopped down flat. Trigga lifted one brow, as he watched her face twist up, and tried to keep his neutral. But inside, his gut twisted. He hated to see her in pain.

"I need to ask you about this man," Trigga said, pushing a photo in front of her. It was the same one that had burned a hole in his mind since the first day he'd seen it so long ago.

Keisha picked up the photo and squinted at it hard as Trigga held his breath. It would be easy for her to say that she didn't remember—she had the perfect excuse—but Trigga knew that she wouldn't lie to him. Would she?

"This... this is Dr. Ishmael," she said finally, her eyes still pinned to the photo as she collected her thoughts. Trigga sat in silence, his poker face intact, although his mind was reeling with thoughts and questions he wanted to ask.

"He's my fertility doctor," Keisha finished and now it was Trigga's turn to frown.

"Fertility doctor?"

Keisha licked her lips and an uncomfortable scowl crossed her face. She shifted in her seat and licked her lips again, letting go of a deep breath before she continued speaking.

"I didn't want to tell you about him because I didn't want you to know that I was trying to get pregnant because of what happened with..."

Her words faded away, but Trigga didn't need her to finish them. He knew that she was thinking of the child they'd lost. No matter what he told her, Keisha blamed herself for not being able to keep their baby alive, and she didn't care what the doctors told her or what medical terms they spewed out. In her mind, her only job as a mother was to keep her children safe, and since she couldn't do that due to her history of abuse, she took the blame.

"I started seeing Dr. Ishmael on my own, to see if he could tell me what was wrong with me. I knew you would say no if I asked, so I didn't tell you about it."

Against his better judgment, Trigga snapped, slamming his fist against the table in his anger. "I would have said no because there is nothing fuckin' wrong with you, Keesh! What happened wasn't your fault. Fucked up stuff happens and that's all there is to it. I don't like you blaming yourself for this shit!"

Tears came to Keisha's eyes, but she blinked them away before they could fall. Trigga saw them anyways and instantly felt like shit for getting her so emotional. But he couldn't help his feelings when it came to her. Keisha was always stressing about whether she was good enough for him, pretty enough, smart enough, gangsta enough... he couldn't wait until the moment she'd realize that she was more than enough.

Under the surface, the guilt of what happened between he and Lania also fucked with his mind, but he pushed those thoughts away for the moment. Since the night they'd narrowly escaped the motel with their lives, he hadn't seen or heard from Lania and he prayed that it stayed that way.

"This picture... why you kissing this nigga though?" Trigga asked, pulling his focus back to the photo that was still in Keisha's hand. She looked down at it and shrugged.

"I'm kissing him on the cheek. I look happy about something but... I don't know, I—"

Before she could finish her sentence, Trigga already had her cellphone in his hand and pointed in her direction.

"Call him."

He watched her face for any sort of hesitation but there was none because, although confused, Keisha was sure that there was no wrongdoing on her part. Keisha wasn't sure why there was a photo with her walking out of the hotel with her doctor, kissing him on the cheek. And the crazier thing about the photo was the timestamp stating that it was the middle of the night. As far as she could remember, she'd never met him at that time, so what was going on?

"Hello? Dr. Ish—"

"Keisha! Are you okay? My office has been trying to get in contact with you for weeks now about—"

"I was in the hospital," Keisha forced out with her eyes closed, not really wanting to go through a game of questions with Dr. Ishmael that she couldn't answer. "I was attacked and in a coma for a while, but I'm fine. And so is the baby." She added the last part when she heard Dr. Ishmael take in a breath. He exhaled it slowly once he was assured that the baby was okay and, for some reason, it relaxed her too. But Trigga's piercing eyes, focused dead center on her face, reminded her of the true nature of her call. Taking a deep breath, she let her eyes cast around the empty living room of their home, and she said a silent prayer that she didn't have skeletons hiding in the closet that she was unaware about.

"I'm so glad that everything is fine, Keisha. That said, I would like you to come in so that we can run some tests to make sure that everything is fine with the baby. We need to continue your appointments as scheduled."

Bending her head down, Keisha looked at the palm of her hand that was covered with a light sheen of sweat and immediately flipped it, rubbing it on the top of her thighs. Trigga caught the slight gesture and felt his chest tighten as he waited for her to continue on with the conversation. True to his nature, he was calm, but Keisha knew that if the wrong information came out of this conversation, Trigga would become a deadly storm that no one would control. And she also knew that Dr. Ishmael would be a dead man.

"Dr. Ishmael, I need to ask you something. I'm suffering some memory loss from the attack and I just need your help with something. D—Did we ever meet at... at a hotel? Like at night?" Keisha bent her head down, unable to meet Trigga's eyes, although she could feel the heat from his stare on her face. She looked at the photo in her hand and, for some reason, began to feel like she couldn't breathe. Just that quickly, the room had turned suffocating.

"At night?! Oh God no! Jonathan would not be happy with me for being out the house at that hour. He calls that our 'couple time!'" Dr. Ishmael chuckled a little on the phone and Trigga clenched his fist tight, still a little on edge.

"We met at a hotel for lunch the day that I told you the good news, but that was the only time we met outside of the office. You were so worried that you couldn't conceive again... so when it finally happened and I got your results back, I asked you to meet me for lunch. We had lunch, you got very emotional—I think we may have caused a little bit of a scene." He laughed and Keisha smiled as if she could remember the moment, but she still couldn't. "But after that, we left and you told me that you would finally share the news with your husband. You said that you hoped it would turn things around for the two of you. That was the last time I saw you, so naturally, I was worried that something happened."

Keisha closed her eyes, releasing a single tear that flowed down her cheeks. It wasn't because she thought she'd betrayed Trigga in some way because she knew that she could never do that to him. But still, it was a terrible feeling to not be able to remember things and moments that were so important; like the moment that she found out she was pregnant again, or even the person who had attacked her. If she hadn't felt useless before, she definitely did now.

"Th—thank you, Dr. Ishmael. I really appreciate it."

"No problem at all," he replied. "Although you are a patient, as you know, I like to think of you all as friends because I'm helping you with something that is so important. I'm helping you expand your family! I would love to assist you in any way that I can. By the way, Jonathan and I are having a dinner party in a couple weeks and would love for you and the hubby to stop by. You know you're my favorite and we have a bit of good news of our own to share."

Keisha forced out a smile and tried to push away the discomfort that still ran rampant in her body, even after she ended the call with Dr. Ishmael. Sure, she and Trigga were now certain that she hadn't been cheating with Dr. Ishmael, but there were still so many unanswered questions.

"Who sent you this?" Keisha asked finally, holding the photo up in her hand. "Someone wanted to make you think that I was cheating on you... who would want to cause issues between us?"

Running his hand down over his face, Trigga molested his facial hair between his forefinger and thumb but didn't readily say anything. He knew exactly who he suspected, but he wasn't sure why the same nigga pressing him for millions would be the least bit interested in his marriage to Keisha. Shit wasn't adding up, and he hated to be in the position he was in where it seemed like he was the last person in control of his own life.

Someone else was pulling the strings, and although he hoped that person was now dead, something told him that his problems weren't that easily solved. Call it the clairvoyant ability that God gave gangstas, or maybe it was simply the paranoia that accompanied street life; either way, Trigga didn't feel comfortable that everything was over.

"Mommy, can I have a sandwich? I'm *still* hungry," Cameron announced, emerging from the hallway, rubbing his hands with his tiny fists.

"What do you mean you're *still* hungry, Cam? You act like you just ate something. You've been napping for over two hours," Keisha said with a giggle to which Cameron simply shot her a confused stare with one brow lifted that resembled one of his father's many expressions. "Why don't you go turn on cartoons and I'll whip you up something for lunch, okay?"

"Okay!" Cameron quipped with a bright smile and ran over to the living room, plopping down right in front of the television. He grabbed the remote and worked it like a pro. In less than a few seconds, he was singing loudly to the theme song of one of his favorite shows.

"I hate that stupid shit," Trigga said under his breath as he watched the yellow sponge gyrate in front of the screen, chiming in his annoying voice about ripped pants. "I don't know why you let him watch that."

"*Let* him watch that? Since when do I *let* Cam's spoiled ass do anything? Like you said, he's a grown man and he does what he wants, just like his father."

Standing up, Trigga walked into the kitchen and stood right behind Keisha, who was whipping up a quick egg sandwich, Cameron's favorite. Breathing in deeply, Trigga sucked in her scent and felt a stirring in his loins that he couldn't ignore. In moments like these, he realized how much he loved his family, how much he needed them with him. He also realized how much he had to get back on the streets so that he could protect them. Trying to keep shit legal did nothing but put his family in harm's way because he couldn't keep an ear to what was going on. Keisha wouldn't like it, but he couldn't play Normal Norman anymore. He vowed a long time ago to live and die by the barrel of his gun, and now he had to return to that life.

Placing his arm around her, he ran his hands over her slightly bulging belly and thanked God for sparing their child. Then he leaned into her neck and took in a deep breath, loving the smell of her shampoo.

"You're so fuckin' beautiful," he said, and Keisha's knees almost buckled from the overwhelming passion she felt within his words.

"Slow down, you know we can't do anything until the doctor clears me," she warned him with a light giggle, but deep down she couldn't wait for the moment when she could feel him inside of her again.

"There are some other things I can do that only require you to sit back and relax," Trigga replied back with ease. Keisha blinked slowly, drunk on his love as his cool breath tickled her earlobe. The eggs were nearly over-cooked, but she couldn't bring herself to pay them the slightest bit of attention when he pulled his hands up and cupped her breasts, squeezing gently, before swiping his thumbs over her nipples and sending chills down her spine.

"Mommy, is my sandwich—Ewwww!"

Keisha gasped and jumped while simultaneously swiping Trigga away from her. She stumbled a little and he chuckled loudly as he grabbed her around the waist to steady her at the stove.

"It's almost done," Keisha informed their son who was standing at the entrance of the kitchen with a mischievous smirk on his face as he looked from his mother over to his father. Behind Keisha's back, Trigga mouthed "this *my* girlfriend" to his son who crinkled up his nose for a minute and then gave his father a thumb's up sign.

"I got one too," Cameron whispered to Trigga, but not low enough for Keisha not to hear.

"Got you one what?" she asked, not looking in their direction as she spread mayonnaise on Cameron's sandwich.

Trigga watched as his son's eyebrows shot straight up in the air before he did an about-face and ran into the living room, distancing himself from the conversation.

"Nothing!"

Trigga couldn't help but laugh at the perplexed look on Keisha's face as she looked from Cameron to Trigga while finishing up her masterpiece of an egg sandwich. It was the first time he'd really laughed, really felt content, in months. Though he knew that the seriousness of his life would most likely take over again soon, he prayed that he'd have more moments like these to celebrate with the ones he loved the most.

12

*L*ania wrinkled her nose at the feet sitting in her lap, covered with corns and cracked, grayish looking toes. And the smell coming from them was even worse, like spoiled pork that had set out in the sun far too long. And she was supposed to *touch* these?

"C'mon, girl! These bunions ain't gonna remove themselves. Hurry up!" her mother ordered, thrusting her foot even closer to Lania's face. She grimaced and then pushed them off her lap, dusting her legs of the 'foot dust' that she imagined may have been left behind.

"Mama, I think you just need to go get a pedicure and let the professionals handle that. Or hell, at least clean them first!"

She watched as her mother screwed up her face and balled up her lips into a tight frown.

"If I wanted strangers touching all over my body, I wouldn't have asked my daughter to do them! After all I done for you and this how you repay me? You left me and didn't even look back, not once did you even call to check on me, but because that crazy nigga you was with after your ass, you wanna come back, and what I do? I accepted you, and *all* my grandbabies I didn't even know I had!"

Blowing out hot air, Lania rolled her eyes and listened for what seemed like the millionth time as her mother reminded her of all the 'favors' she was doing for her. Truth be told, they were favors she wouldn't even be doing had it not been for Lania paying her out the ass simply for providing them all with a place to stay.

After the night that Trigga had shot Austin, Lania knew she had to leave town for fear that Austin would kill her and their children. Or at least their son, who Austin never seemed to think was his to begin with. Her fear was only further confirmed when she received a haunting text from Austin's phone with four words that sent chills down her spine: *I'ma kill you, bitch.*

The only problem was that she had little money left and no way of leaving without help. She was no match for the power that Austin had on his side. He had a countless amount of money at his disposal and a team of men ready to do anything he asked. Being that she knew too much of his business, there was no way he would allow her to leave him with her life. So she called on the only person she felt could help her: Queen.

"What do you want?" was the greeting that Queen gave her as soon as she picked up the phone.

Lania wiped a tear from her eye. Her heart had already accepted the fact that calling on Queen was probably a lost cause. After all, her business with Lania was already done. Lania had successfully distanced Trigga from Keisha, making him more comfortable with going back to the street life where he played the role as Queen's top earner. The problem was, Queen had no idea that Austin was also pulling Trigga's strings, or that Lania was working with him. Now, somehow, Lania had to convince the smartest Queenpin the state of New York had ever seen to help her when there was nothing more in it to gain on her end.

"I need help... I have someone after me and I just need help getting out of the city."

True to her nature, Queen scoffed and rolled her eyes, wondering why it was that Lania thought their roles were equal enough for her to be able to ask for a favor instead of the other way around. That wasn't how Queen operated because she didn't need to. Every action that came from her was self-serving, and how did it serve her to help Lania?

"I think it would be smart for you not to call this line anymore—"

"Please!" Lania called out, tears stinging her eyes and blurring her vision to the point that she couldn't see. *"I have my children with me and...he'll kill my babies!"*

She looked around the small cramped car at her sleeping children, hoping that her outburst wouldn't wake them. It had taken forever for them to fall asleep in the vehicle with the sound of the rain providing them with a soft lullaby. She was too afraid to return to her apartment and find Austin there with a loaded gun full of bullets with their names on them. Trigga may have felt like Austin was dead, but even before she got the text from Austin confirming he was alive, she knew better. Austin had survived the direst of circumstances in the past, and the fact that she hadn't seen a body or heard of his demise, was evidence enough to her that he wasn't dead.

"He'll kill my babies, I just need to get them out—"

"Trigga?!" Queen snapped in disbelief, feeling slightly offended that Lania would even suggest that a friend of hers and someone so high up on her team would ever hurt a child. "Trigga would never hurt a child! Are you crazy?"

"I'm not talking about Trigga!" Lania sobbed hopelessly. "My children's father... he thinks I slept with Trigga. He knows what I did for you and he told me he was going to kill my babies. Please, I just need you to help me this one time. Please!"

Queen went silent but her mind was running. Lifting her eyes, she cut her attention to her own children, Italy and Rome, who were sitting across the room playing with their father, her husband. She had taken so many precautions in her line of business to ensure their safety, but it was still a constant fear that somehow, someone would be able to get to them and hurt them before she could protect them. But the thought of that someone being their own father? She couldn't imagine what a woman had to be going through knowing that the one person who should have shared interest in keeping their children alive, actually wanted to harm them. And Queen couldn't help but feel the slightest bit of guilt that she had played a part in that happening.

"What do you need?" she asked Lania, pulling her attention from her own family in order to focus on helping Lania save hers. "Just let me know and I'll help you... this one time, I'll help you. After that, lose my number because you're on your own."

Queen did help Lania by giving her money and providing her with transportation and security to get her out of the city to the only place she knew of to go where Austin may not find her: her mother's house. Since Lania had run away at the age of sixteen and never looked back, Austin knew nothing about her mother and wouldn't even think to look for her in a small ass non-name of a town in rural South Carolina. So her children were safe and so was she, but there was one problem stopping her from being fully content. She was in love with Trigga.

"Hello?! Nia, snap out that fuckin' daydream so you can tend to my feet, please! I need you to get that lil' scraper over there to file down my bunions and then get them clippers to cut off all that dead skin. My feet been hurtin' like a motherfucka!"

And with that, her mother, Millie, stuck her feet right back under Lania's nose and leaned back in her seat with an expectant look on her face as she crossed her arms in front of her massive breasts. Sighing, Lania picked up the scraper, held her breath and began to do as her mother asked, but in her mind, she was somewhere else, making plans of how she would get back to Trigga. With her kids' safe at her mom's, she knew all she had to do was shoot her some money every now and then to watch them in order to keep her satisfied. That way she could return back to New York and Trigga's arms. Only a fool couldn't see that they had chemistry and that he cared for her. She only needed a little more time to work on him and she knew that she'd have him right where she needed him.

In her deepest of thoughts, she told herself that she needed to stop going after the bad boys, stay in slow ass South Carolina, take care of her children, and live a normal life. But Lania was anything but slow, and the men she craved were anything but normal. She needed a bad boy in her life and Trigga was the one she fantasized about. She realized that her attraction to Austin was based on the power and strength he exuded, but she could get the same with Trigga minus the constant ass whoopings and threatening of her children's lives. Sure, his rough, crazy, and unpredictable nature had excited her at one point, but after fleeing New York for fear that she would wake up to a gun to her head or her babies', whatever love she had for Austin was gone.

If her assumptions were right and Austin wasn't dead, he would contact Trigga sooner or later to make good on the rest of his sinister plan. Lania needed to be by his side when that happened so that she could help track him down, giving Trigga every piece of the puzzle he needed so that she could earn his trust, and eventually... his love.

13

a large shadow fell over Keisha, but instead of tensing up, she relaxed and dropped her head back, feeling even more secure when Trigga's broad, muscular arms wrapped around her. He leaned down and pressed his lips to the top of her head before pulling away to stand in front of her.

"You tired?"

She shook her head before cocking it to the side, seeing a twinkle in his eyes that let her know he had something planned. She licked her lips and darted her eyes over to Cameron, who was sitting on the floor drawing without a care in the world. Surely he could wait until Cameron went to sleep before he acted on his urgings from earlier.

"Good." Trigga's lips curled into a sneaky smile and his dimples popped out on each side, making Keisha have to squeeze her thighs together. It had been so long since she'd felt him the way that only a wife could feel her husband, and she couldn't lie and say that she didn't crave him in that moment. She needed him in more ways than one.

"Good, why?"

"Because in about five seconds, you're going to have company," Trigga informed her and then looked down at his phone. No less than a few seconds after he'd said it, there was a loud knock on the front door, followed by the blaring of the doorbell made by someone who was impatiently jamming their finger against it. Trigga didn't even have to tell her; she already knew who it was before he walked over and opened the door.

"Nigga, why da fuck you pressin' on my shit like you done lost yo' damn mind?!"

"Muthafucka, I don't even know why you still had the damn door locked when I just told yo' ass we was right outside!"

Keisha laughed as she watched Gunplay walk in and dap up Trigga before pulling him into a brotherly hug. LeTavia followed in behind him, pushing Gunplay out of her way so that she could make her way to first, Cameron and then, Keisha.

"Uncle Plaaaayyyy!" Cameron screamed, bypassing LeTavia as if she wasn't standing there. LeTavia frowned and placed her hands on her hips as Cameron ran right up to Gunplay and jumped in his arms, wrapping his tiny arms right around Gunplay's thick neck and long dreads.

"I guess he ain't see me standin' here, huh?"

LeTavia smirked while acting like she was really offended. This was nothing new. When Cameron's uncle Gunplay came to visit, he was all he saw and no one else. LeTavia sat down next to Keisha but kept her eyes on the exchange between Cameron and Gunplay, and Keisha recognized the look in her eyes. She had been trying to conceive as well, but so far hadn't had any luck. Keisha made a mental note to relay Dr. Ishmael's information to her later on so that she might be able to create her own miracle the same way Keisha had.

"So, girl, how you been doing? I mean, other than the obvious... I know it's going to take some time getting physically back to 100%, but you know I'm not talking about that." LeTavia raised both of her brows at the end of the sentence, and Keisha nodded her head before taking a deep breath and looking over at Trigga and Gunplay to make sure they were out of ear range. She knew exactly what LeTavia was referring to.

"It's just hard... I know he wants to pressure me into remembering who did this to me, but I can't. I know it has to be pissing him off at some level, but he's doing a good job about hiding that from me. Still, no one knows Trigga like I know Trigga." Keisha forced out a tight chuckle, her attempt at easing the tension she felt. "He's going crazy not knowing for sure who did this, and it's kinda fucked up knowing that I should be able to help him but I can't."

Tears came to Keisha's eyes and LeTavia reached out to wipe away one that escaped. Deep down, although she would never tell her, she considered Keisha to be her closest friend. They didn't always see eye to eye, mainly because LeTavia saw her as a little spoiled with her head in the clouds, about what life with a nigga like Trigga really was about, but she still loved

Keisha like a sister. Especially since, these days, she didn't get to speak to her own sister much.

"You have to let him get back in the streets, Keesh," LeTavia advised in a soft tone, continuing on even after Keisha stiffened. "The reason that Trigga is so out of it right now, the reason he doesn't know shit is because he was out so long. You have dated two niggas in the game and you still haven't comprehended that there is no way to just get out and act like you were never in it. You always have to keep an ear to the streets... it's the only way you can watch your back. You think convincing him to get out protects you, but it doesn't. It only makes Trigga vulnerable to shit like this. Now his ass gotta play catch up."

Keisha frowned lightly and ducked her head, trying to hide the single tear that had formed in the corner of her eye. Everything that LeTavia said, she had thought of herself. Every single word. Truthfully, she blamed herself in more ways than one for the position that she'd put Trigga and their family in. She just didn't know how to fix it. But once again, LeTavia seemed to know her thoughts.

"Talk to him. He's under a lot of stress right now. Nothing fucks with a man's mind more than knowing that someone was able to touch their loved ones." LeTavia paused and looked longingly over at Gunplay, who was engaged in his own intense conversation with Trigga, and Keisha knew she was thinking of her own relationships problems as well. "You have to let him be the man he is, the man he's always been. You can't change a goon into a gentleman because it suits you. When you married him... you *married* a goon."

Sighing deeply, Keisha nodded her head and swallowed down the bitter pill that LeTavia was feeding her, but she knew in her heart that she was right. Not once had Trigga ever tried to change her from who she was, and not once had he ever put pressure on her to be anything more than what she was used to being. He accepted her flaws and he dealt with them. Couldn't she do the same for him?

On the other side of the room, in hushed tones that could only be heard between the two of them, Gunplay was dishing Trigga some real shit of his own.

"That's fucked up how Keisha keep getting her ass whooped, nigga," he said with one brow raised. Trigga felt his chest burn but didn't immediately say anything. After all of the years of knowing Gunplay, he was used to the fact that Gunplay had a peculiar way of putting things that could in fact lead to him getting his own ass beat.

"I'ma find out who did it," Trigga promised with more confidence in his tone than he'd actually felt.

"Oh?" Gunplay quipped before sipping from his glass of Hennessey. "You got any leads?"

He asked the question but he knew the truth was that Trigga was just as lost as a nigga walking around drunk in the dark. If he had any leads, one thing was for certain: they wouldn't be here chatting, sipping and shit while discussing it. They would be out in the trenches, preparing to pull the trigger on one unlucky nigga.

"I told you I thought it was Austin... Lloyd's cousin from Texas. But after your contact out there said he ain't never left the city, now I see it's somebody trying to confuse the shit out of my ass."

"And it looks like they're succeeding with that shit."

Trigga clenched his jaw tight, and Gunplay read from the look on his face that he needed to pull back on his natural asshole nature. After blowing out a deep breath, he placed his glass down and fixed his eyes on Trigga who he regarded as an older brother and mentor, though in this instance, he was acting like anything but. When Trigga was on his shit, he was *on his shit*. But stepping away from the game had him fucking up in ways that Gunplay would have never predicted. And although Gunplay knew that Keisha was the cause for all of that, he knew better than to place any blame on Trigga's wife.

"Listen... we can work together and find this nigga, but you gon' have to be all in from here on out. I'm tired of this half-assing shit where I gotta put my shit on hold to help yo' ass but when I need a shooter, you playin' Daddy Marcus the law-abiding citizen, ya dig? You either all in or all out."

Without saying anything, Trigga glanced over at Keisha and drained the brown liquid in his glass, pushing out hot air as he felt the burn. He'd already made a decision to go back so what Gunplay was saying wasn't even needed. His mind was set and whether or not Keisha decided to ride through it with him was up to her, but his decision was made.

"Aye, nigga, I'm all in, and I decided that shit some time ago. Keesh might leave me for it, but that's just the price I have to pay to keep my family safe. She'll understand one day."

Nodding his head, Gunplay affirmed that he agreed with Trigga's words. No matter how much he loved LeTavia, she would find herself sad and alone if she ever tried to get him off the block. It was in him and it was how he was when they met. He didn't know any other way to get it other than from the muscle, and he'd be damned if anybody tried to pull him away from his first love: the streets. He was the king of the underground and that's how he would stay.

"In the meantime, you gotta show her ass how to shoot a gun or somethin', nigga. You can't keep lettin' niggas wipe up the floor with her ass. This shit is vicious out here, and these niggas don't give a fuck if they gotta snatch ya baby, murk ya baby mama, or kill ya moms. They will do that shit, and you gotta make sure that when you ain't around, your shit stays protected."

"True shit, nigga. I'ma do just that. She ain't never wanted to have to shoot a gun, but it's not her decision anymore. I want to make her happy, but her idea of being happy is pretending that niggas ain't out here still wanting to repay me for shit I've done in the past." Trigga paused and, once again, his thoughts went to Austin who also had a few things he would have probably wanted to repay Trigga for.

For one, after they teamed up to kill Austin's cousin, Lloyd, Austin came back weeks later and sent word that he wanted Trigga to return some of the money that Trigga had stolen from Lloyd's traphouses before his murder. Seeing as Austin was now over them, he saw it as a direct assault against him and figured that since he'd helped Trigga get rid of Lloyd, he owed him some of the money back. Of course, Trigga refused and started his club from the money, but he didn't think Austin seemed like the type to let bygones be bygones. But would he really want to wage a war with Trigga after all this time?

"You *sure* your contact over there in Dallas is reliable? Austin hasn't been out of Dallas at all since all this shit has been happenin' with my fam?"

"Nigga, what I'm tellin' you is that I asked a broad about this nigga and she not only said that he been there but she went to the club this nigga stay partyin' at and took a pic of his ass when he rolled through. The chick thorough as hell... she tryin' to get on my good side because I stopped fuckin' with her and she been tryin' to get a nigga back. She ain't got no reason to lie. Austin ain't the one who hit you, B. And the more you think on that nigga, the more you givin' whoever really did this time to come back around and press you again. I don't know why they haven't already. Unless you really did kill that nigga."

Shaking his head, Trigga let his eyes run across the room and fall on Keisha, who was laughing as she spoke to LeTavia. He wished that he felt that was the reason why, but he didn't.

"Naw, I don't know about that. I didn't see a body so I can't say I did. Until I get proof that this shit is over with, it ain't over."

14

"When does the homeschool teacher come?"

Trigga walked into the kitchen where Keisha seemed to be standing in one place, deep in thought, and sat down on the barstool in front of her. In what felt like no time, she'd gotten stronger and was standing on her own without the cane. His words pulled her out of her head and she jumped slightly before letting her eyes settle on his face, which was pulled tight in a concerned frown.

"In about thirty minutes. Cam is brushing his teeth and getting dressed now, then I told him he could watch TV before she got here. I was just about to cut up some fruit for him to eat before she gets here."

"Good," Trigga replied. "I want to take you somewhere after they get started."

"I'm nervous about leaving him alone..." Keisha's voice trailed off and Trigga knew what was on her mind, but he couldn't help but snicker.

"This woman has been vetted by Queen and a team of security is escorting her over here and will stay while she's teaching Cam. Not to mention, the security system I got on this shit is so official that God Himself is the only nigga who can get through. Ain't nothin' gon' happen to that big head boy of yours, Keesh. Not ever again."

Standing up, Trigga walked over and wrapped his arms around his wife, knowing that their son's security must have been what was on her mind when he had first walked in. Just the fact that she was worried about shit like that messed with him in ways that he couldn't stand. The last thing he wanted was for his wife to be worried about the safety of herself or their child. That was his burden. He just wanted her to be happy and to live life without fear.

Soon enough.

"I love you, Keesh," Trigga whispered his words across the nape of her neck, and Keisha shivered, closing her eyes as she relished their closeness. No man on Earth had that effect on her, and none would.

"We got thirty minutes, you said?" Trigga asked, and Keisha nodded her head, knowing exactly what he was up to.

Scooping her up in his arms, he opened the door to the large walk-in pantry behind them and backed into it, kicking the door closed once they were inside. He didn't bother turning on the light because he wasn't worried about seeing; he only wanted to feel. And he couldn't wait to feel all of Keisha, all of the things that were his and his alone but had been taken away for so long.

"I still have another week to go," Keisha purred out her warning but truly hoped that he would ignore it because she had to have him just as much as he had to have her.

"I'll be gentle," Trigga promised and simultaneously released himself from out of the prison of his sweatpants. Keisha had already felt him pressing against her thigh, and a pool formed between her legs as she anticipated feeling him inside of her. It had been much too long already. She wasn't sure how she'd lasted this long.

"Tell me if I'm hurting you," he whispered, but before she could respond, he'd lifted her short dress, pulled her soaking wet panties to the side, and slipped in, in what felt like one single motion. Keisha's mouth formed a perfect 'o' as she took in his width, rolling her hips around to adjust to his size. He filled all of her, and it felt so good that it brought tears to her eyes. They didn't move for a few moments and just reveled in the feeling of being one once again. But then Trigga couldn't take it anymore.

"Fuck!" Trigga gritted and began pushing into Keisha gently but deliberately while holding her hard around the waist.

It was taking everything in him to exercise some self-control and be gentle, when what he really wanted to do was fuck her hard for every moment that he needed to be inside of her and had to deny himself the pleasure. She felt so good to him, so soft, warm, and tight, he could barely get his thoughts together. And then when she wrapped her arms around his neck and started riding his dick, speeding up the pace, he knew then he was about to lose his fuckin' mind.

"I need you, baby. I want all of you," she begged in his ear, and he almost lost control at that exact moment.

Rearing back, he slid out and pushed all of his twelve inches straight into her, hoping that he wouldn't hurt her but unable to tell himself to stop. She gasped and he halted for a second until he realized that it was a moan of pleasure. She clasped her arms tighter around his neck and rode him hard as he jammed his dick steadily inside of her, over and over and over until they both exploded. Keisha's legs went limp around him, and he placed her gently down on the floor of the pantry, lightly pushing her knees apart. There was sweet nectar between her thighs and he wasn't about to let up until he was able to lap up every drop.

She let out a low, long moan when she first felt his cold tongue swipe through her slit, and she flinched slightly before melting into his mouth. Trigga drank from her like she was a fountain gushing honey. He took all of what she had and brought her to another peak of pleasure, leaving her convulsing against his tongue as he rapped it hard against her clit, just the way that he knew she loved it. By the time he was done, she wanted nothing more than to fall asleep right there on the pantry floor.

"Take your time getting up. I know you're tired." Keisha could hear the smirk on his face through his tone. "I'll clean up and get breakfast together for our son."

About an hour later, Trigga was pulling up to the gun range. He hadn't told Keisha where they were going or why, but after placing the car in park and shutting it off, he reached in the back seat and grabbed a black box. Keisha watched him without saying a single word, but when he opened the box to reveal the chrome metallic .44 caliber pistol, she couldn't help but gasp.

"This is yours," Trigga began as she just stared at the gun. "Never again will I allow you to go somewhere without your own protection. We're here so you can learn how to shoot it. And I know you said you didn't want to have to deal with things like this, but it's our reality and I'll be damned if I let you walk around without knowing how to protect yourself."

Licking her dry lips, Keisha reached over and grabbed the pistol from out of the box. She didn't want to admit it, but she felt a surge of power when she held it in her hands. Weak and stupid was how she'd been feeling the last few days, knowing that she'd been attacked and having no idea who had done it to her. She felt so weakened by her lack of knowledge to the point that she couldn't bear to leave the house, thinking that whoever had done it the first time would do it again. But the gun gave her a sense of power she didn't have before.

"Thank you," she said and Trigga nodded his head, willing himself to ignore the tears in the corner of her eyes.

Inside of the gun range, Trigga went first, showing her how to load her weapon, cock it, and shoot it. Keisha watched with eager eyes but also admiration of the level of skill that Trigga possessed. He held, in his hands, a tool that could end a life, but he operated it with such expertise and confidence that it set her whole body on fire. He was a natural-born shooter and she couldn't believe that she ever tried to make him be something different.

"Your turn," he said, handing her the gun. Keisha immediately raised it and took aim.

"Do it like I told you—Keesh! How the hell you gon' shoot a fuckin' gun with your eyes closed?" His question was followed by his thunderous laughter, and Keisha opened her eyes, bashfully ducking her head as Trigga took the gun from her to demonstrate once again.

"You can't shoot shit with your eyes closed. Squint one so you can see better, aim and shoot. You got it?"

She had it. Trigga handed her back the gun and Keisha followed his directions to the 'T,' shooting everywhere but the target, which made him laugh, but Keisha wasn't a quitter. She continued with it for hours on end until she was more comfortable with holding a gun and more precise with her shots. Not once did Trigga complain about how long it took; he stayed right there by her side, coaching her until she was finished.

"Now I need to tell you something," Keisha informed him as soon as they got in the car.

She had a long first day of target practice, but Trigga had signed her up for training once a week with a professional at the range, and also walked next door to sign her up for self-defense classes at the dojo. She wasn't fully clear for exercise yet, but Trigga was eager to get her back on her feet.

"Oh?" Trigga replied to her statement, raising one brow up as he glanced in her direction.

She had her face pulled tight in a thoughtful expression and there was a thin sheen of sweat on the top of forehead, although it was already pretty cool in the car. He wondered if maybe he'd overworked her too soon after her leaving the hospital and made a mental note to make her rest once they returned home.

"I don't want you giving up things for me anymore." Keisha lifted her hand to stop Trigga when he opened his mouth to respond. "I don't want you giving up the person you are... that's what I mean. I knew what I was getting into when we got together. I knew who you were when I married you, and I don't want to change you. I'm tired of this being a battle between us. It's like you're forced to keep secrets because you're trying to make me happy, and I don't want that anymore. You don't have to tell me what you're doing out there, but you don't have to lie about it any longer either. You don't have to hide money or make decisions without me anymore. I vowed to be your partner in life, and that's what I want to be."

The sun shined in Keisha's eyes as she spoke with sincerity, and Trigga couldn't help but think about how beautiful she was in that moment and how connected they were to each other. Even before he had to break the news of his decision to return to the streets, she had already accepted that she was going to let him do what he needed to do. She was the perfect woman; she was *his* perfect woman, and he couldn't believe that he'd almost fucked that up for a temporary thrill with Lania. He thanked God Lania was gone and hoped that his secrets had disappeared with her.

Leaning over, Trigga kissed Keisha gently on the lips, spreading hers apart with the tip of his tongue before pulling away. Then he sped out of the parking lot of the range and headed home. With her blessings, he knew now there was nothing stopping him from getting back in the game, and he wanted to start tonight.

15

"**Y**ou headed out, boss?"

"Hell yeah," Austin replied to one of his hit men, J.D., while staring at the evidence of the injuries he'd suffered weeks ago, courtesy of Trigga.

While most of Trigga's gunshots had been warded off by the bulletproof vest he'd been wearing, he'd gotten some lucky shots in that had actually penetrated his shoulder and lower torso, making Austin lay low for a while until he got his shit together. Naturally, he chose to recuperate in his city where he could be sure that he'd be well taken care of in his vulnerable state, but now that he was almost at 100%, he was ready to get back to New York and finish what he started.

But now, he had more enemies than he'd started with. Lania was nowhere to be found and she was a liability that he couldn't afford to have. Being that she'd been by his side for years, she knew too much to be kept alive. He still couldn't wrap his head around how she'd decided to double-cross him after being his main chick for so long.

What *was* it about this Trigga muthafucka that had the hoes switching sides after being thorough with a nigga for years? Austin didn't know and he didn't care to find out. He just wanted a bullet through both of their skulls. First Lania, and then Trigga after he'd gotten what he was going after—and that was something known only to him. He'd learned a long time ago that you couldn't trust hoes to know your full plan, and Lania's betrayal was evidence of that. It stung that he didn't have her in his corner anymore, but he had a decent replacement for the time being.

"Hey, daddy," Karmen cooed, walking over and wrapping her arms around Austin's neck. She planted a kiss on his lips and he kissed her back while running his hands around her back side to give her tight ass a squeeze.

"Wassup, lil' mama. Where you been?"

"I booked our flights and packed our things so we could be ready to go when you're ready to head out. I know you're eager to get shit started again."

"Fa sho," Austin replied, running his finger over the thin triangle of hair under his bottom lip. "Yo, whatever shit you packed, leave it here. You been good to daddy these past few weeks, showed you a down ass bitch, and I want to thank you for that shit. Soon as we hit the city, I'll break you off with some bread so you can buy all new shit. Good?"

Karmen squealed and jumped in Austin's lap, straddling him right in front of J.D., who stood nearby. Lifting his nose in the air, J.D. turned the opposite way and tried to hide the scowl on his face as Karmen and Austin embraced. Deep down, he couldn't trust the bitch because he knew her for what she was: an opportunist. There wasn't a dick that she hadn't tried to sit on in order to make her way to the top, but finally she'd gotten the right one and Austin was giving her some play. Although J.D. knew that Austin wasn't serious about her and would blow money on any chick he was fucking without really giving a shit about her, it still bothered him that he would waste his time on Karmen when Lania had been the real prize.

"Yo, J.D., I'ma go get ready to peel out this bitch. You and Karmen can get in the car and get shit ready to go. I'm tired of sittin' around letting mutha-fuckas waste my time. I got moves to make, and money don't wait on no man."

Austin sat up, pushing Karmen off his lap, and straightened up his clothes before walking in the back to clean up and get ready to go. The moment he was out of range, Karmen whirled around and pinned her eyes on J.D. with her hands on her hips.

"Our things are in the master bedroom, but you can empty all of my clothes out of the bag except for one of the outfits since *my man* said he'll be buying me all new things," she ordered with a haughty tone that didn't move J.D. one bit.

"Bitch, you get your own shit," J.D. snapped. "I work for Austin, I don't work for you. Thot ass bitch," he added under his breath as he turned to grab Austin's things.

"You work for Austin, *my man*, which means you work for *me*," Karmen clarified as she walked steadily behind him, her heels clicking hard against the tile as she struggled to keep up with his long strides. "Don't get this shit twisted. I'm your boss now and you'll do whatever the fuck I say or—"

J.D. whirled around at lightning speed and grabbed Karmen by her throat, cutting off the air to her lungs as well as the rest of her sentence. She stared at him with her eyes gaped open as if she were looking at a ghost.

"Or what?" J.D. snarled through his teeth. "Or you gon' tell your boss how you used to gobble up my dick the same way you do his? Or you gon' tell him about how you used to fuck around with his deceased cousin and run your mouth to Lloyd for Gucci bags and Fendi dresses?"

Karmen's eyes nearly bugged out of her skull, and J.D. couldn't help but laugh at the surprise and shock in her eyes.

"Oh, you didn't know I knew about that shit, huh? Well, dig this, I know more than you think I know. You're nothin' but a slimy ass bitch who'll double cross your own mama for some dick if you think it'll fill up your pockets, and one day soon, Austin will find out about you."

With that, J.D. released Karmen, roughly pushing her away with so much force that her head knocked against the wall behind her. She lost her balance and fell back, plopping down on her ass, but kept her eyes on J.D. as he delivered his last demand.

"I suggest you get your own shit, bitch. I ain't touchin' it, and Austin is ready to go."

As she watched J.D. walk down the hall towards the master bedroom to collect Austin's things, she knew right then that she needed to get rid of him and get rid of him quickly. He was the one obstacle in her plan that would ruin her dreams of becoming a kingpin's wife. When J.D. had grabbed Austin's bag and was on his way out of the door to pack them into the car, Karmen made her way to Austin to begin working her magic.

"Do you trust J.D.?" she asked, twirling one of the long tendrils from her Malaysian bundles around her finger. Austin was in his office counting up stacks of money when she walked in. His initial thought was to slap the shit out of her for entering into his office without him asking for her, but the question on her lips gave him pause. Always a sucker for the mention of possible betrayal, Austin took a bite of her bait and replied.

"Yeah, da fuck you mean? That's my nigga. Why?"

Twisting her lips to the side, Karmen opened her mouth to speak and then seemed to hesitate, shutting it suddenly as if in thought. The heat from Austin's glare told her that she needed to stop with all the games and speak up before he made her regret even opening her mouth.

"Well, you know he's always wanted what you had. It's no secret that he's always sitting around waiting for you to fuck up so he can move in and be the big boss, instead of only running shit when you ain't around. Even with Lania..."

Karmen paused and her eyes widened as if she'd accidentally begun to say something that she hadn't meant to reveal, but it was all part of her devious plan. She pressed her lips tightly together and dropped her eyes away from Austin's face, but she knew that he'd heard exactly what she started to say and knew, by the way his breathing seemed to become heavier, that he was hooked.

"What about Lania?" he queried in a rough tone, and Karmen almost felt a little regret in bringing her name up.

It was obvious that Austin still held some feelings about her, whether good or bad, from the way his shoulders squared up and tensed at the mere mention of her name. Although Karmen knew that Austin had mentioned on many occasions that he wanted her dead, she still couldn't help feeling jealous about the fact that she felt he didn't really want her harmed but actually back by his side, playing the position of his ride or die... the position Karmen was bent on playing for the rest of her life. It was bad enough that he was always pushing her to accept the things that Lania accepted from him: the threesomes, the abuse, and the fact that she wasn't the only one wanting to be his only one.

"Well, J.D. has always wanted Lania to be his. Actually, I think that he and Lania had a fling once..." She stopped speaking when Austin banged his fist hard against the top of his desk.

"That *bitch*! I knew that fuckin' ugly ass kid wasn't mine!"

Karmen could barely hide the smirk that was teasing the corners of her mouth. She knew for a fact that all of Lania's kids were Austin's, but there was no way in the world she would correct his line of thinking. Especially if it meant that he may spare Lania's life. In her mind, Lania was always getting the best of everything just because of her looks, intelligence, and whatever other tricks she was laying on niggas. It was finally time for her to step to the side so Karmen could get some shine.

"Yeah, truthfully, I always thought that kid was J.D.'s—"

"Then why the fuck you ain't ever open up yo' fuckin' mouth and tell me that shit?!" Austin gritted on her, turning his anger towards the only other person in the room. Karmen took a step back when he came from around his desk with his fists balled tightly at his side.

Shit!

This was not going according to her plan. But that was one of the dangers of dealing with a gangster as unpredictable as Austin with a temper so tumultuous, he would turn on you in a second. His anger had no bounds, which meant that when it surfaced, it was about as containable as lava flowing from a volcano. It destroyed anyone in its path without regard to one's innocence or guilt.

"You over here perpetratin' like you down for a nigga, but you just as flaw as that bitch! During that time, you was fuckin' with me, but you didn't even tell me shit 'bout that bitch and—"

Karmen held her hands up and took a step back, stumbling a little as she tried to distance herself from Austin's fury.

"No! I only suspected that she was fuckin' with him. She swore that she wasn't and that all of her kids were yours, so I didn't have anything to tell. I know how you roll and I ain't wanna come to you on some 'I think she might' kinda shit. I had to be sure and I wasn't, but either way, I know that nigga can't be trusted because he said some shit to her to let me know he was jealous and was just waiting for the right opportunity to move in on you."

Austin's face remained tight, but Karmen knew that she had him thinking hard about what she was saying. Although J.D. had never given him a reason to doubt his loyalty, the curse of living the street life is that you could never be too careful and you could never trust anyone because it was always the ones closest to you who would turn on you. Austin knew better than to take any warnings of betrayal lightly, and although he knew that Karmen wasn't a trustworthy person her damn self, evidenced by how easily she'd willingly straddled his dick while calling Lania her best friend, he knew that she was money hungry enough to always want to stay on his good side.

Maybe this bitch ain't lyin', Austin thought to himself as he stroked the short hairs on his chin.

"And also, I have some good news," Karmen continued, eager to continue showing her worth to Austin. "I think I may know where Lania is. The only other family she has is her mama who lives in South Carolina. I bet that's where you can find her hiding. She doesn't have anyone else."

"That lyin' bitch told me her mama was dead!" Austin snapped, squeezing his hands back into fists. Karmen licked her lips and tossed her long black and brown tresses behind her back with the utmost satisfaction. She enjoyed seeing the murderous intent in his eyes when it came to Lania. It let her know that she was doing a job well done.

"Yeah, it's a lie. She tells everyone that same sad story for sympathy, but really her mama kicked her out on her ass when she was sixteen for being a hoe. You know she slept with her stepdaddy, right? She's always been a nasty little bitch."

"But you were her homegirl, right? You couldn't have thought all that shit back then," Austin replied back for no real reason other than to shut Karmen up. He wasn't one to sit and listen to shit women said just because they were jealous of the next bitch. If it didn't pertain to him, he didn't care.

Before Karmen could recover from the sting she felt from Austin's words, J.D. walked into the office after knocking and letting himself in. Holding back a satisfied grin, Karmen cut her eyes to Austin, sending him a pointed look to remind him of their conversation, before stepping to the side to allow him in.

"Aye, boss, got you loaded up and ready to go. I'll hold it down until you get back and send you updates every week... same shit as always, a'ight?" J.D. informed Austin, deliberately ignoring the way that Karmen was boring right into the side of his face, her brown eyes pinned on him as she waited for Austin to put him in his place.

"Yeah, I'ma need you on somethin' else, so I'ma put Loki in charge for the time being. Looks like that bitch, Lania, is in South Carolina living with her moms, and I need you to find her for me."

J.D. started to chuckle incredulously, a dry laugh like he couldn't believe what Austin was saying.

"You wanna put Loki in charge of what? That nigga ain't been here long enough to prove his ass is thorough enough to be over shit. Especially to be in charge of the Dallas Hittaz. The DH crew don't move for no nigga who ain't put his time in like—"

Before J.D. could get another word out, Austin had pulled his glock out from his side and was gripping it so tightly that his knuckles had paled. With one smooth flex of his index finger, he dislodged the safety, and J.D. stood in front of him frozen like a statue as he waited for Austin's next move.

"The fuck you talkin' what the DH crew ain't gon' do for, nigga?! I put that crew together and they gon' do whatever the fuck I tell them to do! If I tell them to take orders from a nigga, they gon' take orders from that nigga! Fuck you think? That this shit can't run without you? That's what kinda time you on right now?"

J.D. was confused by Austin's sudden outburst as well as his demotion out of the position of power he was used to enjoying as the second in charge. Not just that, he'd asked him to conduct a mission that was usually reserved for the lower level niggas in the crew. He'd put in too much time for Austin to be sending him on a mission to find his ex-bitch. J.D. was seething just thinking about it, but he knew enough not to let it show. Angering Austin was like poking the devil and daring him not to wreak absolute havoc. It was just stupid to do.

"Whatever you want, boss. I'll call Loki and let him know what's up."

"Naw, I'll call that nigga and let him know what the fuck I need him to do with my muthafuckin' team. You do what I asked you to do, and I expect to hear back soon. Shouldn't take that long to find that bitch. She ain't that fuckin' smart," Austin replied back, dropping his head dismissively as he started pecking at the screen of his phone.

It was then that J.D. finally turned and saw the malicious smirk on Karmen's face, which spoke volumes. It was obvious to J.D. that somehow, she'd managed to get in Austin's head. With a curt shake of his own, he turned around to walk out. If Austin wanted pussy to control him, then so be it. In J.D.'s mind, it was about time he started working on building his own name. If a bitch could come in between the relationship that he had with Austin and change it up in a matter of minutes, Austin may not be the type of nigga he wanted to work with anyway.

"Aye, you ready? It's time for me to get back in the city. Got shit I need to finish," Austin said, still pointing his full attention to his phone.

"Yes, daddy," Karmen replied back as she stood up to go grab up her luggage bag and the few things she intended to take with her. This time, she went to get her bags without the attitude. She may have lost the battle when it came to J.D. playing the part of her personal servant, but with him almost out of the picture, it was obvious that she was winning the war.

16

*L*ania puckered her lips and spread her red cherry blossom lip gloss over her lips before admiring her appearance one last time. After confirming that Austin was back in Dallas, she didn't hesitate to take the next Greyhound bus back to New York City so that she could convince Trigga that she was the woman for him. It had only taken her a brief day or so of mental tug of war, for her to decide it was time to leave her babies with her mama and win Trigga's heart for herself. The fact that her mama was anything but an accommodating houseguest and was always reminding her how much she needed to get off her ass and get a job didn't help matters either. So here she was, back in the city, sitting in the back seat of a cab as she prepared to find her way back in Trigga's life.

There was only one problem: his wife. But Lania had decided that even if she was no longer in the hospital, she couldn't have recovered enough to give Trigga all the things that Lania knew he needed. Even before going into the hospital, she was coming up short when it came to pleasing her man, so she would be an easy problem to overcome.

"Thank you, how much do I owe?" Lania asked the cab driver to which he simply pointed to the number on the meter, clearly annoyed by the fact that she'd been sitting in the car primping in the mirror for the last fifteen minutes.

Rolling her eyes, Lania tossed him over a few crumpled-up bills, leaving only a small bit of change for his tip, and jumped out of the cab. He sped away so fast and suddenly that he nearly removed a few of her toes in the process. As soon as Lania set foot in the club, all eyes turned on her. Even so, there weren't many eyes to turn as the club was only half full. From the look of it, Trigga had put Yadi back in charge and she'd let everything go to shit in only a few weeks. The music was thumping—thankfully the DJ was still on point—the strobe lights were setting the mood, and the chick on stage, a stripper by the name of Cherry, was working it on the pole. Still, there was not really an audience to speak of.

As Lania stood at the front of the club near the doors, she felt a rush of wind when the doors parted and she turned around, coming nearly face-to-face with one of the hottest rappers out. Her mouth almost dropped to her beautiful blue glittered toes as she watched him stroll in like he owned the place, with an entourage of about twenty niggas walking in behind him.

"Oh my fuckin' go—is that Lil' Wa..." Lania couldn't even finish her sentence as she looked at him and the group around him, many of them other rappers on his same label. She sucked in a breath and thought back to a time in her not-so-distant past when she fantasized about dancing for him one day and twirling her fingers around one of his long dreads.

"Damn, this shit look ghost as hell up in here! What da fuck Trigga got goin' on? This spot used to be the shit when I came out here some years ago," he fumed, and Lania hopped out of her daydream, panicked about the fact that the largest client the strip club had probably seen in a while seemed like he was about to go.

"Yeah, we need to hop to that spot across the way. I told you that shit over there looks like it's lit as fuck! I heard they got lions and shit in there."

"Yeah, but my nigga from way back owns this spot, and I wanted to show him some love. Shit... is that nigga even here?"

Tossing his dreads behind his back, he took one last look around the club and started to turn as if he were about to leave, and that's when Lania jumped to intervene. Standing up straight, she pushed her bountiful bosoms into the air, poked her ass out behind her, and walked quickly behind him, grabbing him lightly on his arm to get his attention.

"Hey, I know you're not leavin' so soon, baby," she cooed in her sexiest voice, walking around until she stood right in front of him. On the inside, she thought that she might faint but on the outside, she fought to keep her composure. Instead of getting a response from the focus of her attention, however, it was his sidekick that stepped forward to answer.

"Well, bitch, you thought wrong because this shit whack as hell in here. We goin' cross the way where they got some real shit goin' on."

Lania bit down on the inside of her cheek to stop herself from snapping at the midget man with too much mouth who was addressing her, and kept her attention on the real man in charge.

"If you stay, we'll pack this shit up in less than thirty minutes. And for the first hour, you and your crew can drink for free and the V.I.P. room is yours, courtesy of the club," Lania continued, twisting her wide and curvy hips to the beat as she spoke, trying her best to hypnotize him with her beauty. He didn't speak, but he didn't look away either.

Point number one for the stripper bitch, Lania thought to herself.

But then the fat mouth to the side of him had to speak up again.

"Bitch, money ain't never been no muthafuckin' issue for us! Do you know who we are? You know who da fuck *he* is?!" He jabbed a fat finger at the leader of their crew, but Lania still ain't bat an eye because she was too busy speaking to him with hers.

"Aye, I don't really care about all that shit but I 'preciate the hospitality," Lania's crush spoke up finally, and Lania gushed, squeezing her knees tightly together to stop them from knocking. "Really, I just wanna holla at my nigga, Trigga. I ain't seen him in a while and was trying to swing through so I could holla at his ass. Damn, look like business down bad though."

He looked around, finally pulling his attention away from Lania to look around the nearly deserted club, and she got anxious once again.

"I'll get him out here. At least stay and enjoy your drinks... if shit ain't poppin' by the time your free hour is up, then you can leave. By then, it'll really be turning up across the street anyways. Just trust me, you won't regret it," Lania all but begged as she pushed her tits even higher in the air. She was well aware that she wasn't the only bitch with nice breasts that he could get to do anything he wanted, but she prayed that she would be able to work some magic to get him to stay.

"A'ight. One hour, and I'm only doin' this because this my nigga's spot and I wanna holla at him before I fly out in the morning."

Grinning widely, Lania tried to hold down a squeal as she turned around to lead the crew to the V.I.P. lounge, while sexily twisting her hips from side-to-side with each step. If Lania thought that every eye in the club was on her before, it definitely was now, and she relished the attention. It didn't take long for word to travel around the club that they had a celebrity guest, and before she could even make it to the V.I.P. room, girls were surrounding them, begging to entertain whether they were paid entertainers or simply guests of the club. After getting them situated in the V.I.P. lounge and ordering two girls to send them over two bottles of Ace of Spades, Lania grabbed her phone to send off a text to Trigga.

Hey, this is Lania. I'm back at the club and you won't believe who I have here with me. You're about to make some major money.

She sent the text off and bit the inside of her lip, hoping that Trigga would respond favorably and not cuss her ass out for disappearing on him for the past few weeks without a trace. About a minute later, she saw the bubbles pop up on the screen indicating that Trigga was replying to her text.

Where da fuck have you been?! And what you mean I'm about to make some money?

Grinning, she read his message feeling that it was his special way of letting her know that he had missed her, said in his normal aggressive manner.

Check the club's IG and FB page. I put up an announcement. And, by the way, you need to get here because he asked to see you.

The idea of putting up social media pages for the club was another genius idea that Lania had brought about and was a way that she had business booming when she was over the club. After she left, it looked like no one cared to keep it up, but she knew from the constant notifications she was getting on her phone that her photo of the rapper and his entourage at the club was getting a lot of hits. In less than a few minutes, everybody who was over at The Gentleman's Club across the street would be traveling over to the club to party with a celebrity.

Shit! I'm on my way, was Trigga's response, and Lania smiled, licking her lips before locking her phone and heading to the locker room. Trigga was on the way and that meant she needed to make sure she was dressed damn near in her birthday suit to remind him of everything he'd been missing since she was gone.

Just like Lania had predicted, in less than an hour the club was packed, popping, and *lit*. Trigga had come through about a half hour after she called him, and had even convinced the main attraction to do a few of his hit songs on the stage while the girls all got together and did a show reminiscent of something seen in Nelly's "Tip Drill" video. Everywhere you looked, hood niggas and trap stars were tossing money in the air and there were women everywhere helping them do it. Standing back, Lania crossed her arms in front of her chest after wiping away a little sweat from her forehead. She'd just finished up her fifth dance that night and was about to go in the back to freshen up and change, when she decided to take a minute to admire her work. Yadi had been shooting her stank ass looks the entire night, but not even that could steal her joy. She had proven to Trigga that she was an asset to his team and couldn't wait until he took a moment to stop mixing and mingling with the crowd so that she could have some one-on-one time with him.

"So I owe all this to you, huh?"

The voice came from behind her and instantly drew a smile to Lania's soft lips. To her, their connection was crazy. She'd been thinking of him and, out of nowhere, he arrived as if her thoughts had summoned him to her side. They were meant to be.

"I wouldn't say you owe me," she replied, turning around to meet his beautiful gray eyes. "But I won't shoot you down if you try to make it up to me."

The comment caught Trigga off guard, but instead of instantly putting her in her place as he would have done any other woman, he let it go with a dry chuckle thinking that she had earned the right to drop an off-color remark or two. Thanks to her quick thinking, she'd packed the club to max capacity. They were even turning niggas away and there was a crowd gathering outside partying in the parking lot. Even with her letting over twenty niggas in V.I.P. drink for free for an entire hour, he was making enough profit in a day to cover what they normally made in a week.

"What you need to do is explain to me why you left," Trigga pushed, cutting right to the chase.

It was nice having Lania back, and the fact that Keisha didn't remember how much she'd hated that he hired her to begin with was an unintended plus, but he still had questions about how she'd so easily left him high and dry after he'd taken her shitty-smelling ass home.

"I had to get my kids to my mama's. After what happened, I just didn't feel safe in the city anymore. I know I didn't have anything to do with what was going on," she added quickly to cover her own ass. "But I just think about what would have happened to them if something had happened to me. I don't have anyone here and I needed them to be safe."

Safety of one's fam was definitely something that Trigga could identify with. He'd have done the same thing to save his own.

"I get that. But next time just let a nigga know somethin', a'ight? We a family here and, for real for real, if anything happens to you, I got you. We wouldn't leave ya kids hangin', feel me?"

Lania nodded her head as she stared dreamily in his eyes, getting lost in them with every passing second. He was such a beautiful man, but the deadly side of him—the side that no matter what, he could not hide—only added to his allure. That thug appeal was something that Lania couldn't deny her attraction to. It was what had made her want Austin so badly the first time she saw him, but he was too savage for her. She preferred a man like Trigga, who saved his savage ways for the streets, and not for the woman who shared his bed and birthed his children.

Damn, I can't wait to have his babies. Lania couldn't help the thought from crossing her mind as she took a minute to admire his features. The two of them together would be a beautiful thing. They already had formed a great partnership in the club; now she needed to be his partner in life. And there was only one thing standing in her way.

"I feel you and I appreciate that, Trigga. How are things at home? I heard Keisha's out of the hospital. It's gotta be hard being there for her after everything, huh?"

The mention of Keisha warmed Trigga's heart but also stung him with a bit of guilt, as he thought about the fact that he was standing here talking to the woman that he'd almost cheated on her with, when Keisha had been doing everything in her power to simply give him another child. The weight of his bad decisions felt like an anvil tied to his neck, and he instantly felt the urge to get away.

"Naw, she's good. No issues at all," he said in a rush, his eyes looking everywhere but Lania's face. She frowned heavily, noting the change in him and regretting the fact that she mentioned his wife.

"Wait..." Lania grabbed his hand to pull his attention back on her and Trigga paused, a soft frown crossing his face.

"Yeah?"

"I just—I just think there is nothin' wrong with us being friends, ya know? We're partners and I just want to do everything I can to help you. You can ask me for anything..."

Trigga didn't reply right away but he definitely saw the lust in Lania's eyes, the way she arched her back to lift her breasts into his face and also the way she licked her lips suggestively. Chicks like her were poison, thrown in the game to shake a nigga's life up for the worse. Although he appreciated her business sense, he knew better than to spend too much time around her.

"Aye, lemme holla at you later. I'ma bounce around and make sure everybody good. Thanks again for lookin' out."

And with that, Trigga walked away after addressing her like she was any other employee who worked the club instead of the woman who would be his future wife. His future everything.

"Fuck," Lania cursed as she watched him walk away.

So close but yet so far. She had to think smarter if she was going to get Trigga because she could see that his loyalty for Keisha ran deep. Why, she didn't know. From where Lania stood, the bitch wasn't good for anything at all.

"Hey," Lania called out, grabbing one of the girls as she walked by her.

Her name was Choice and she was the gossiper of the crew. She had a bad body, complete with a fat ass and was young as hell, or at least she looked that way, which had old ass, nasty perverts spending all their money just for a second of her time. But the reason that Lania wanted her was because the girl always seemed to have the latest gossip and she loved to tell it. You didn't even have to give her anything for the news either, she was just eager to tell it.

"What's up, Nia. You back, huh? These bitches out here was sayin' that Trigga fired yo' ass for havin' somethin' to do with his wife bein' attacked because y'all sleepin' together, but I knew that was a lie."

Twisting a lock of her hair around her finger, Choice popped her gum as she scrutinized Lania's face for any hint of a reaction. Lania fought the urge to roll her eyes, knowing that Choice was the main bitch spreading the lies.

"Damn, girl. Bitches be sayin' all kinds of stupid shit these days," Lania half-joked, loving the way that Choice struggled to push away the guilt-ridden look in her eyes. "That ain't why I left at all. Trigga and I are on *very* good terms." Lania's words were covered in thinly veiled sexual insinuations, and Choice's eyes widened in pleasure. "But... what happened with his wife? She still alive, huh?"

Choice laughed, tossing her head up to the ceiling as if it was the craziest thing she'd heard. "Yes, girl, she's still *alive*! You so crazy. And the baby is alive too... but word is, that bitch can't remember shit. Whoever beat her ass beat the memory clear out of her. She can't even remember who the hell attacked her!"

"What?!" Lania replied, playing her role in the exchange.

"Yeah, girl. Crazy shit for real. And then I heard that Red was killed too! They said it was somethin' drug related and—"

"Yeah, I don't wanna hear about that shit," Lania interrupted with a wave of her hand. The last thing she wanted to think about was the sight of Red's bullet-riddled body and missing face from where the bullet had blasted her. Just the memory of it stirred her stomach.

"Damn, was y'all tight or somethin'?" Choice asked, fishing for more gossip. It was like a switch that she couldn't turn off. She was always looking for a story.

Bitch should've been a reporter in another life.

"Naw, not really. But I'll talk to you later, girl. I'm about to go run this money up."

Before Choice could say another word, Lania turned around and walked away, her mind running with different devious plans that she could put into work with the additional knowledge she gained. Keisha's loss of memory was probably the best thing that happened to Lania in a long time. She knew the perfect way to get closer to Trigga and to get Keisha out of the way.

17

"So what do you have planned for the club tonight?" Keisha asked Trigga as she stroked Cameron's hair while he slept on her lap. After begging and pleading to stay up late to watch *Transformers*, he fell asleep in his mother's lap only an hour in, just as she and Trigga had predicted. Even so, they decided to finish the movie on their own.

"My nigga made a few calls, got some up and coming rappers to stop by and either perform or just make an appearance. I called on a few celebrity rappers and hood niggas I've connected with on some business in the past too, and asked them to swing through," Trigga informed her with his face tight. By this time, Keisha was able to see right through him to the things he wasn't saying.

"I know you don't like to ask people for help, Trigga, but you know *a lot* of people who could help you turn this club around. It's okay to ask them to stop by to draw a crowd. It's not a show of weakness to pull a few strings and ask for a few favors when you need it."

Trigga didn't look at her but accepted her words with a nod. She was right and he knew it; still, he hated asking for favors. He hated that fact that he couldn't do this shit on his own. Still, he knew that Keisha was right. He could have turned this club around a long time ago and avoided a lot of shit they went through, if only he'd pushed his pride to the side.

"When you became so fuckin' wise?" Trigga joked, chuckling a little when Keisha cut her eyes at him as if asking 'when wasn't I?.'

"That's something I was blessed with from birth. It's just hard to get yo' thick skull ass to listen to my wisdom."

"I guess my thick skull goes with your thick ass."

One half of Trigga's lips lifted into a smirk, and he couldn't help glancing down at the top of Keisha's breasts that were showing from out of the top of her low-cut shirt.

"Humph," Keisha grunted, rolling her eyes at him, but he could see the smile teasing her lips as well as the way her breathing seemed to slow as he continued to stare at her. She was trying to keep her lil' fake attitude going, but he could see through it all and wasn't the least bit convinced.

"Don't even be lookin' at me like that because you ain't getting none," she teased.

"Nigga, I'll get what da fuck I want. Believe that."

Trigga licked his lips, loving her sassiness. It was a sign that she was getting back to her old self. Looking down, he eyed her growing belly and felt a warm feeling fall over his body. She didn't have much but a little bump, but still, he was struck with a little bit of happiness, paired with a little bit of worry, knowing that his seed was growing inside of her. He prayed to God that nothing would happen to their baby. Already their child was a trooper like its mama, surviving through the crazy circumstances that led to Keisha's long hospital stay.

Just thinking about it made Trigga's chest get tight. Someone had touched his family, his *wife*, and no matter what connections he and Gunplay had, they were no closer to finding out who was behind it all. He knew he had to play his position and stay patient. He knew that mutha-fuckas like the one he was dealing with couldn't stay down for long so he'd resurface again, but Trigga would be lying if he didn't say he was looking for that shit to happen soon.

Leaning over, Trigga kissed the top of Keisha's head and pulled her closer into him, running his arm around her shoulder, just as his phone began to vibrate against his hip. Reaching down with his other arm, he grabbed it and thumbed through to his messages.

Gave you long enough so now it's double or nothing. Next time I hit you up, you better have 4 milli waiting for me.

Trigga read the text and then stuffed the phone back in his pocket, careful not to alarm Keisha or let her know anything was wrong as he retreated into his thoughts. Although unexpected, the text wasn't a surprise and he couldn't say that he didn't see it coming one day. He'd learned long ago to never underestimate an opponent, but also that unless there was proof, never to presume someone as being dead. Still, as he thought out a plan of attack, Keisha's words ran through his mind.

It's not a show of weakness to pull a few strings and ask for a few favors when you need it.

As much as Trigga wanted to do this alone, he knew that he had to think smarter for the sake of his family. He had to call in a few favors from a few key people who could help him get shit in order.

"So you need weapons... a lot of them. Are you planning some war I don't know about?" Queen asked before sitting behind her desk in her luxurious office.

It was obvious, just from taking one look around, that there was no expense spared, and one would think that was because Queen required it that way, but it was far from the truth. Her husband, Dre, was the one who had demanded everything around her to be that way. He adored Queen and it was obvious in the way he took care of her.

"Shit, I don't plan for it, but if it goes that way, I'm muthafuckin' ready."

"And what's in it for me?" Queen inquired with a cool tone, asking the single question that Trigga knew she would.

Regardless to how long they'd known each other, Queen made it clear that business was business and it was separate from whatever other relationship they shared. She didn't mix the two, but Trigga preferred it that way. If he asked for something, he liked to earn it and make the deal an even exchange.

"We can continue the old agreement. If you got somethin' that needs to be done, let me know and I'll handle it for you."

Queen pursed her lips like she was thinking on it for a moment, and then countered his offer.

"Is that it? I can't convince you to officially join the team?" she pressed. Trigga shook his head.

"I don't do teams."

Queen wasn't surprised at his response, the same way that Trigga wasn't surprised at her inquiry. This was the same song and dance they'd been engaged in for over a decade, when Trigga first left from being her personal bodyguard and shooter and decided to go on his own.

"One of my men got picked up by the FBI," she informed him, and

Trigga raised his brows at this. It was no secret that Queen had many key members of the Feds on her payroll, so for any members of The Queen's Cartel to get picked up was odd to him. Queen pretty much operated without even giving a thought to the local police because she'd been able to either bribe or blackmail anyone who had enough pull to fuck with her. And she had the same pull when it came to the Feds but, every now and then, someone new was put in charge and decided to flex his muscle. That must have been the case this time.

"The reason he was picked up is because he was doing his own business on the side and got caught up. With me unwilling to protect him, he may say too much... do too much damage for me to cover up. So he has to go."

"It's done," Trigga spoke with finality and confidence. Queen looked at him, her eyes shining with appreciation, something that she reserved only for her closest friends.

"It should be easy but it won't be. He's being held upstate and I haven't been able to get much information on it. That lets me know they are protecting him so he's already been talking. For that reason, it's going to be difficult to get to him, especially after the last hit you did for me. This job pays a quarter mill."

"I would have done it for free," Trigga replied honestly. "Regardless to what happens, you know my loyalty is with you because you've always been loyal to me."

Nodding her head, Queen pushed a long tendril of her black hair from her face, and it was then that Trigga noticed that her caramel complexion was tinged with a little red on her cheeks. There was a thin layer of sweat on her forehead although it wasn't hot in the room and she, all of a sudden, wouldn't meet his eyes. It wasn't like her to seem this way. She was always so collected and well put together. Trigga looked away, feeling discomfort at seeing her in a state he wasn't used to.

"Andre will help you get any guns you need," she said finally nodding her head towards her husband who was sitting a little behind Trigga reading a magazine. Then Queen sat down in the chair at her desk and sighed deeply. When she looked up, she seemed back to normal, and Trigga chucked up her flushed face from before to some female shit that he wouldn't understand.

"I also need security at the club and more at my crib to watch over Keesh and Cam. I don't want shit happening while I'm gone."

Queen nodded her head curtly and pressed her lips into a thin line. "Whatever you want, you got it. Just kill him and do it quickly. He's one of the ones that will get the best of you if you give him time, so get it done as soon as you get a good shot."

A light flashed through Trigga's eyes before he turned around to walk out of Queen's office, Dre stood as well, placing the magazine down so that he could get Trigga the weapons he needed.

"Not happenin'. I'm done with muthafuckas getting the best of me."

18

"Oh! Are we goin' to the club?" Karmen quipped as soon as she looked out of the window and saw the large, flashing sign that read 'The Gentleman's Club.' Reaching over, she turned up the volume of the radio in Austin's dark blue Maybach and started twerking her hips in the seat to the sound of a Future song.

"Fuck no! And don't touch my shit!" Austin spat, cutting the music down before balling up his fist and raising it to Karmen. Her eyes widened right before she shrunk back in her seat, holding her hands up over her face as she squeezed her eyes closed.

"Don't mess up my makeup, please!"

Pausing, Austin looked at her and almost felt the urge to laugh at her stupid ass. He'd been known to dislocate jaws, and here she was begging for him to spare that clown shit she had on her face. If nothing else, Karmen was comic relief, but he still couldn't understand why he kept her around. She was nothing like Lania, and the fact that he had to put up with her instead of deal with the real thing made him want to kill Lania even more. It was twisted to think that he missed someone so much that he wanted her dead, but Austin had never been one to think with a sane mind.

"Just sit back and shut the fuck up," Austin ordered Karmen before turning his attention back over to Trigga's club.

From where he was, sitting in his car surrounded by his own security team of gangsta niggas, he could see that Trigga had stepped up his own security as well. The entire club was surrounded from the outside to inside by Queen's security team. You could tell they were members of The Queen's Cartel just by looking at them. Only her men would be wearing tailored suits like they had stepped out of GQ Magazine, but be covered in tattoos and carrying AKs and shotties like the SWAT team.

But this was all proof that Austin's plan was working out nicely. Now he had solid evidence that Trigga was back working with Queen because, if the rumors were true, Queen didn't extend favors without issuing demands of her own. Austin also knew that when she needed her dirty work done, she'd call on her most trusted shooter to help. Until recently, Trigga had been reluctant to work with Queen but like anyone, all he needed was to be put in a position where he didn't have any other choice.

For years, Austin had been trying to get his hands on Queen because he knew that if he could take over her empire, he'd be unstoppable. He wasn't the type of hustler who could build his own from the ground up. He was the type who waited for another nigga to build it up and then take it from him by force. He'd done the same with his cousin, Lloyd, and now he ran the entire southeast region of the country. He'd done it even before that, when he took over Texas, and he planned on doing it again now... with Trigga's help.

Queen was untouchable. She moved in shadows and had a team of men who would die to protect her. By the time someone spread the news that she was seen somewhere, she was gone without a trace. Her moves were calculated with the most perfected precision. No one knew where she laid her head at night except for her most trusted members of The Queen Cartel. The problem was, no one knew who the most trusted members of The Queen's Cartel were, so it was nearly impossible to extort them for information. But then there was Trigga. The one member of her innermost circle who was allowed the right to operate on his own but still have access to her. So while Queen was untouchable, Trigga was not, and Austin knew Trigga would be his way to Queen.

Austin's phone began to ring and he pressed the button in the car to answer over the Bluetooth speakers.

"Aye, boss... anything you want us to do?" Thinking for a minute, Austin crafted out the rest of his thoughts in his mind before replying. Now that Trigga was fully back in business with Queen, it was time to take his plan up a notch. He'd been patient enough... waited too long. He couldn't wait any longer.

"That nigga ain't in there or he wouldn't have all these other muthafuckas surrounding the club. He's too proud for that shit," Austin said, vocalizing his thoughts. "That means he must be working with Queen to find Nauti. After he kills that nigga, follow his ass back. Let me know when he gets back in the city."

"You want us to kill him?"

Austin's eyes almost bulged out of his head.

"Why da *fuck* would I want you to kill him?! I said follow his ass, nigga!" He roared so loud into the speaker that Karmen flinched slightly at his side. He cast a menacing look in her direction, remembering that she was still there.

"Well... you ain't really tell us what you got planned for the nigga, so I was just askin'—"

"Don't ask nothin' fuckin' else. Just do what I told you to do, and call me when that nigga hits the city. Take one car; the rest of them niggas need to stay with me. We gon' have an early celebration at The Gentleman's Club."

Karmen squealed, jumping up in her seat and clapping her hands at the thought of being able to party. So far being the main chick to a thug had been boring as hell, but she knew all of that was about to turn around because when Austin decided to party, he *really* partied. There were bottles popping, money flying, and he gave her everything she wanted. She could get used to that kind of life, even if she had to deal with the beatings and crazy erratic behavior that came with it.

"Shut da fuck up!"

Karmen was in the middle of clapping and dancing her ass against his black leather seats, when Austin backhanded her like she was a man. Her head knocked back hard into the window to the side of her, and she felt a sharp pain erupt through her forehead.

"You better not have fucked up my shit, bitch!"

Austin snatched her roughly by the neck, pulling her away to examine his window as Karmen bit down on her bottom lip to hold in her moans of pain. She didn't want to do anything to upset him and make him hurt her even more. She hadn't learned yet, that Austin's pleasure came from inflicting pain, and the fact that she was holding in her cries only made him want to beat her more. Winding her hair around his fist so tightly that he nearly pulled a track from her scalp, he used her hair to wipe up the brown smears of makeup that her forehead had left on his window.

"Owww, that hurts!" Karmen cried, tears stinging the corners of her eyes. But Austin only ripped harder, twisting her head up so that she could look him in his eyes.

"You think I fuckin' care?"

A single tear slid down her cheek but she didn't say a word. He was holding her too tightly for her to even shake her head to respond. Times like these made her wonder if all this abuse was worth it. But when you've never had nothing, even a little bit of something was enough to scare anyone into dealing with a lot of shit. Karmen was one of the unlucky ones born into poverty and abuse, only escaping it by the skin of her teeth and the warmth of her pussy. But out of all the men she'd fucked in order to survive, her own father included, Austin was the only one who provided her with the life of a celebrity. It was money, clothes, and fast cars every day with him, and she couldn't leave it alone only to have nothing in return.

"I'm sorry," she apologized, allowing many more tears of pain and worry that he wasn't done abusing her, to escape her eyes. With each tear that fell, Austin's dick grew harder and harder. It wasn't the same as with Lania; Lania loved the pain just as much as he loved inflicting it. But still, the sight of Karmen crying only made him want to fuck more tears out of her.

"Get in the back," he said, releasing her hair. Confused, Karmen squinted up at him, resisting the urge to rub at her tender scalp.

"Huh?"

"I said get in the fuckin' back seat! And take off whatever shit you got on under that short ass dress."

Unable to slide through the middle because of the partition separating the two areas of the car, Karmen unlocked her door and took a deep breath. There was no telling what Austin was up to. He went from hot to cold in a matter of seconds. He was unpredictable, wild, and savage to the core.

Without another word, Karmen stepped out of the car, opened the back door, and slid into the spacious back compartment of the car. Seconds later, Austin joined her, a crazy, insane sparkle hidden behind his eyes. He was a gorgeous man, but if you looked in his eyes for any real length of time, you could see the demons that lie beneath. Glancing down, Karmen saw that he was holding his long, thick, anaconda dick in his hand, stroking it hard, priming it for entry. As if he hadn't just beat her ass with the same hand only seconds before, she let out a lustful breath and felt her pussy gush honey. It was hard to not react that way to Austin's pretty rod of pleasure. But pleasure for Karmen was the last thing that Austin had on his mind.

Before Karmen knew what was going on, Austin grabbed her roughly by the shoulders and flipped her body around. Then he gripped inside the hook of her hips and pulled back, arching her body so that her ass was up. He positioned himself behind her and plunged first in her pussy, wetting his dick with her sweet and sticky juicy juice before pulling out and smashing the head of his dick straight through her anus.

"Arrrrrgh!"

Karmen's mouth stretched wider than the Grand Canyon as she let out a howl that could wake the dead. She felt her insides splitting in two as Austin pelted his hips forward, pushing in and out with all the vivaciousness of a nigga on speed as she wailed in pain.

"Yes, bitch, take that dick!" he chanted as he jerked every bit of his twelve-inch long and nearly two-inch thick penis into her.

She felt liquid dripping from her and she knew it had to be blood and God knew what else. A stinging sensation made her entire body tense up as he continued to impale her, and she knew that he'd broken the skin. Tears streamed down her cheeks, right into her open mouth, as she continued to cry in pain and misery. But it only seemed to excite Austin all the more, and he started pumping hard, throwing his dick into a circle, ripping her ass to shreds as he coached her all along the way to 'take that dick.'

Is it worth it? was the question that came to mind, said in a voice that wasn't her own. She recognized it as Lania's, almost as if she were speaking to her through her own head, taunting her for her decisions to betray the person who was supposed to be her best friend.

I said, is it worth it? The voice came again and Karmen squeezed her eyes shut, wincing hard when Austin slapped her on the side of her ass and then ripped at one of her nipples, nearly pulling it from her breast.

"No!" Karmen screamed loudly before gritting her teeth together in painful agony. She lifted up and brought her hands to the side of her head, covering her ears as if to silence the noise. "Noooo!"

"Da fuck you said, bitch?!" Austin snapped, punching her in the back of the neck and making her fall back into the arch that he wished her to be in. "You said you can't take this dick?!"

Karmen didn't utter a single word as Austin continued piledriving her ass, pushing into her like he was digging for the answer to her question his damn self. Dropping her head, she muted her cries by biting down hard on her arm and tried to ignore Lania's voice still echoing in her head.

Is it worth it?

19

"Aim and shoot!" Keisha's instructor told her, and she did exactly as she was told without a shred of fear. Squeezing her eyes closed, she imagined that she was pointing her weapon at the face of the person who had beat her, kidnapped Cameron, and almost killed her unborn child, and then opened her eyes and squeezed the trigger.

Pow!

Pow! Pow! Pow!

"Whoa! Hold up!" Reggie chuckled, rapping his fingers lightly against her arm. "I only said shoot once. You're getting a little overzealous, huh?"

Keisha flashed him a small smile and shrugged her shoulders lightly. "I guess I'm just a little tense." Reggie shot her a knowing look, raising one brow as he nodded his head in understanding.

"You've been through a lot the past few weeks. I get the reason you're tense, but I'm here to help you make sure nothing like what happened ever happens again."

This time, a genuine smile crossed Keisha's lips, and Reggie couldn't help but notice the way that his dick thumped against his jeans.

Damn, she's fuckin' beautiful, he thought before looking away.

He knew better than to lust after Trigga's wife. Although he had developed an attraction for Keisha over the few weeks they'd been working together every single day, his respect for Trigga was greater than his craving for his wife. But his desire to live trumped all that. No matter how much

Reggie knew about guns and how precise a shot he was, he was nothing in comparison to Trigga. He had a command on any weapon in his hand that was unmatched, insane even. He was *ill* with it. And Reggie knew that Trigga wouldn't hesitate to showcase his skills by delivering a bullet to his dome if he ever crossed the line with Keisha. So he kept his admiration of her tucked away in the back of his still intact head.

"Should I shoot again?" Keisha asked after a few seconds of silence passed, and Reggie nodded his head, pointing with his finger to the full-body dummy ahead of them.

"Yes. This time no head shots. You're good on those. Try the other kill shots and if you can nail them, I think it's time to let you work the obstacle course."

Keisha's eyes lit up and she turned to look at Reggie, wondering if she really heard what she thought he'd said.

"You think I'm ready for that?!" she shrieked, and Reggie laughed heartily, nodding his head.

"To be honest, I think you've been ready. Your skill is on point and you've been working hard at this. You know the basics, so all that's left is to put it into action," Reggie informed her, trying hard to keep his feelings at bay.

For some reason, it was incredibly hard today. It could be because of the fact that he hadn't had sex in a while or it could have been the fact that Keisha was wearing a pair of short shorts that showed off her beautifully toned, slender toffee-colored legs. Either way, his dick was doing all kinds of acrobats in his pants, and he was mentally tired of trying to will away his growing erection.

"Thank you!" Keisha shouted and jumped up, pulling Reggie into a friendly hug.

Although he felt a certain way about her that she was unaware of, her feelings for him were nothing more than as the brother she always wished for and never had. However, the bulge in his pants that she felt against her leg after she enveloped him in a hug told her that he thought otherwise. Keisha gasped and stepped back, instantly feeling like she'd done something wrong but unsure of how to handle the awkwardness of their situation.

On the other hand, Reggie was mortified and wanted to kill himself for even allowing his body to react the way it had. If Keisha ever mentioned any of this to Trigga, not only would his friendship with Keisha be over, but so would the bond he had with Trigga, and possibly even his life. It was hard to predict Trigga's mind state these days or how he might react to something.

He was always on edge. But Keisha knew this too and didn't want to be in the middle of any additional problems for her husband.

"Okay, so for those kill shots," she started, turning back to the dummy before checking her weapon to make sure she had enough rounds available. "This should be easy."

Reggie agreed, laughing nervously, but happy that she had managed to change the subject.

"That's right. Nothing big because you've definitely already got this. Just aim and shoot," he said. Pushing the events from only a few seconds ago from her mind, that's exactly what Keisha did.

After practice was over, Keisha still wasn't able to fully move on from what had occurred between she and Reggie, and it made her want to see Trigga immediately. After going out to work the night before, he told her that he needed to do something with Queen and would be working through the night. Now it was the next day, and other than a few text messages to stop her worrying and to make sure she and Cameron were alright, she hadn't heard from him.

This wasn't something that wasn't normal. Keisha had learned long ago that when you were in love with a man who dealt with the streets, you played second to the block. She never allowed that to bother her because she trusted Trigga with her own life, and she knew that if he didn't come home, it wasn't because of another woman. But something was bothering her and it had to do with the fact that Reggie, who had a wife of his own— one that Keisha actually liked, was attracted to her. And she couldn't help feeling that if she allowed him to act on his attraction, he would happily take it there with her.

With her still recovering, in addition to the stress she knew that Trigga was dealing with, they hadn't shared many intimate moments at all. In fact, the quickie in the pantry had been the first and only time they'd even had sex since she'd been back home. And before her hospital stay, they'd been apart, so Trigga, a man whom she made sure was getting pussy on the regular for over five years, had been going months without.

The fact that he worked with sexy women every day, worked closely with them the same way that Reggie did with her, had her mind playing tricks on her. And she also couldn't ignore that her memory seemed to be slowly coming back, bringing to her remembrance a conversation she had with one of the girls at the club—she couldn't remember which one—who had warned her about Trigga being with a certain other dancer. So now the question in her mind was...had he really been working all night or was he *cheating* on her?

Keisha walked into the club slowly, feeling as if she were coming in for the first time, although she'd been there so many times before. But this time was different. She felt like everyone around her knew things that she wanted to know but they'd probably not tell. Their loyalty was always to the boss, Trigga. If he were doing anything, they wouldn't tell her. Although she'd gotten close to a few of the girls, the relationships weren't genuine. It was only because she was the boss's wife and for no other reason. They were cordial but not very friendly.

"Hey... Yadi, is Trigga here?" Keisha stopped the woman right as she strolled by her, hand-in-hand with a man that she was undoubtedly about to service. He cut his eyes at Keisha, obviously annoyed at her delaying his pleasure, but she ignored him and placed her attention on the curvy, sexy, and scantily clad woman standing by his side.

"No, I haven't seen him," Yadi said with a shrug, her tone seeming a little more aggressive than Keisha expected. She wondered if something had happened between them that she couldn't recall.

"But maybe you should ask *Lania*," Yadi added with a strong roll of her eyes. "She's the one your lil' husband put in charge after demoting me from managing the club. She should know everything, I guess." Another eye roll but Keisha only squinted, confused at what she was saying.

"Lania? Who is that? And what do you mean that she's managing the club?" Keisha asked, slightly annoyed that Trigga hadn't told her that he had a new woman in charge after informing her that B.J. had been killed. It seemed like he'd put her up-to-date on nearly everything except for that.

"She's the new chick that Trigga hired." It was obvious from Yadi's tone that she couldn't stand Lania and Keisha wanted to know why. "But anyways, let me get to work because your lil' man ain't been giving a damn about the mouths I got to feed since he ain't worried about me getting no extra hours. I gotta make the most of what I can get."

And with that, Yadi sauntered off, swishing her big ass behind her and leaving Keisha with the feeling that she should have checked her for calling Trigga her 'lil' man.' It wasn't no secret that Keisha and Yadi never really got along, but she'd always respected Trigga. Until now, it seemed.

"Don't let her bother you. She's just salty, but what's new?" a voice said from behind Keisha and she pivoted quickly.

When her eyes landed on the beauty in front of her, she wasn't quite sure how to react. She was a gorgeous woman with a beautiful butterscotch complexion and straight black hair, cut into a long, layered bob, which was similar to the one that Keisha was now sporting herself. She was almost an exact replica of Keisha except that she was covered in beautifully crafted tattoos and donned a much more toned body; something reminiscent of the curves that Keisha flaunted back in the day when Trigga had first met her, before the multiple pregnancies had widened her waist and brought about stretch marks that she struggled to hide.

Pursing her lips, Keisha thrust her hand forward while keeping her eyes on the woman in front of her who stood nearly in the nude, wearing only a pair of gold, sequined shorts that were cut like a pair of panties, and a thin bra-thing that covered nothing but nips alone.

"You must be Lania. I'm—"

"Keesh!" Lania began to laugh like she'd just heard the funniest thing on Earth. "Are you really going to act like we don't know each other?"

Before Keisha could react, Lania pulled her into a hug, pushing her barely-covered breasts against her chest.

"Sorry, I just don't remember, uhm..."

"OH!" Lania exclaimed, smacking her forehead with her hand while widening her eyes. "It must be the memory loss! Girl, we are the best of friends!"

Screwing her face up, Keisha frowned deeply wondering what in the world she could possibly have in common, besides looks somewhat, to make her want to be the best of friends with Lania.

"We are?" Keisha questioned her and didn't bother to hide her suspicion with Lania's declaration.

"YES! Girl, you're the one who told Trigga to give me this job! He was all thinking that you wouldn't want me around because... well, because you know how you can be when another pretty bitch is working around your man!"

Keisha's eyes fluttered as she fought to ward off the stinging sensation in her chest as she took in the truth behind Lania's words. She was right, Lania was just the type of woman that would raise both of her eyebrows if she were to see her working one-on-one with her husband. So why would she have ever convinced him to hire her, and allow her to manage the club at that?

"Trigga wasn't going to hire me, but then you saw me crying and I explained about how I had to feed my children. And... then I told you about the miscarriage." Lania's face dropped and Keisha felt her own heart tug at the mention of the 'm' word.

"Miscarriage?" she asked and Lania nodded her head.

"Yeah... my boyfriend beat my ass and killed my baby. I moved here to get away from him and start a new life on my own with my kids. After I told you about it, you told me about how you'd lost...well, you know."

Lania stopped there and shrugged, allowing Keisha to finish the sentence for herself. Truth was, Lania didn't even know the whole story of what had happened with the child that Keisha had been pregnant with before her current one. Trigga had only let it slip that she'd been pregnant before and lost it before he was able to remember that he didn't want Lania privy to his personal business. Still, his partial admission was enough for her to go off on.

"I'm so sorry to hear that," Keisha lended in a hushed voice, thinking on Lania's words.

They made perfect sense because, knowing what she'd been through and how she felt about her own son, she would never allow Trigga to turn a woman away who was trying to provide for her children, simply because of her own inner issues with jealousy. And, true to her character, once she heard Lania's story of what happened to her and everything she'd gone through, she would have definitely begged Trigga to help her.

"It's okay, girl. I know that you're just trying to get your memory together. I can't fault you for that."

Then something occurred to Keisha and she frowned once again, placing her suspicion-filled eyes into Lania's.

"But if we're such good friends... why haven't you called me or been by to visit since I've been out the hospital?"

But Lania had an answer for that too. After being with Austin for so long, she was a quick thinker, if not anything else.

"I just got back in town. I had to leave to take my kids to my mama's down south. I found out that my boyfriend had followed me here and I was scared that he would hurt them. I just got back a couple days ago and asked Trigga if I could come by to see you because I have a new phone and didn't have your number saved. He told me to give you some more time to get yourself together first."

Nodding her head, Keisha accepted her response because she had no reason not to. And it was just like Trigga to stop people from visiting, unless it was Gunplay or LeTavia, two people he was close to as well. He was so protective of her in that way.

Licking her lips, Keisha took a deep breath as she remembered her reason for being at the club in the first place. She needed to speak to Trigga.

She needed to be sure that he wasn't stepping out on her. If she gave him the freedom to roam the streets at night, she wanted to make sure that the only thing she had to worry about was him coming back home safe and sound—not him being in the arms of another woman.

"Is Trigga here? Or... has he been here this morning?" Keisha asked, bringing her sad eyes up to Lania. She couldn't find the strength to hide the pain she'd feel if she found out that he had been with someone else. Lania's own eyes registered with alarm at Keisha's question.

"No, I haven't seen him... He hasn't been here since some time last night. Why, is something wrong? You think something happened to him?!"

Keisha was too caught up in her own feelings to realize how worried Lania seemed to be over a man that wasn't hers.

"No, I just—I haven't seen him since last night and..." She let her words fade off before she said too much. She was much too smart to allow a woman she barely knew, regardless of the friendship they *allegedly* had, know the innermost worries in her mind when it came to her marriage.

But Lania was smart enough to pick up the words Keisha hadn't said and knew that she was worried Trigga was stepping out with another woman.

Shit, he better not be, unless it's with me! she thought to herself, feeling a tinge of jealousy of her own rattling within her chest.

"No, the last time I saw him was sometime last night, but then he left with Toy," Lania lied. Truthfully, she hadn't seen Toy since she'd been back. She assumed that she might have been one of the ones who was now working over at The Gentleman's Club.

"Toy?!" Keisha repeated, eyes nearly bulging out of her skull as she visualized the dark-skinned beauty that went by that name.

"Yeah... they left together, I think. But, it's not anything worth mentioning to him, girl. It was probably nothing, and you don't want to seem like that crazy jealous type. Men hate that shit," she added, seeing that her words were already working through Keisha's mind. She had her right where she wanted her and she could tell it, even though Keisha was trying hard to hide it.

"I'm sure it *was* nothing. But if you see him, can you tell him I stopped by?" she asked and Lania nodded.

"Of course I will! Bye, babes!"

Lania watched as Keisha walked away, fighting back a laugh at how easy it was to manipulate Keisha's fragile mind. Poor girl didn't know what to think or believe. She was open game for any and everything, which made it that much easier for her to get rid of so Lania could have Trigga for herself.

20

*K*armen sat on the floor with her head in her hands, trying to get over the throbbing pain shooting through her rectum as she listened to the fuck sounds coming from the other side of the wall. If she thought that she was miserable after Austin had invaded her from behind, she was mistaken; what she felt now was true misery.

After nearly an hour of fucking her in the ass, Austin pulled out and wiped his dick with her dress before muttering that she get herself together and join him in the club. With dried tears crusted up on her face, her hair torn all over her head, and her dress smelling like her own ass, she eventually joined him inside only to be further humiliated.

Niggas like Austin weren't a dime a dozen, but the thirsty ass females who loved them were. And when Karmen walked into the V.I.P. room that Austin was occupying in the club, Austin had nearly a two dimes' worth of them surrounding him, either running their mouths over every part of his body, sliding their hands all over his skin, or twerking it out all over the room to provide him with the best kind of entertainment. One girl had her mouth stuffed with his dick and Karmen frowned down at her as she nearly gobbled it whole. Upon seeing Karmen's face, she mistook her disgust for jealousy and winked as she unknowingly continued sucking the remains of Karmen's ass from off of Austin's erect dick.

"Sick bitch," Karmen had said under her breath... or at least she thought she had. Apparently, the girl heard it and decided that, although she wasn't too good enough to be sucking the skin off some unknown nigga's dick, she was too good to be called a bitch. She released Austin's pole from her mouth, making a resounding noise, *pop*, and screwed up her face at Karmen.

"What da fuck you called me, bitch?!" she roared, and Karmen looked back at her, unwilling to bow down as a few of the other girls stopped what they were doing to watch.

"I called you a sick bitch! Why don't you tell me how my ass taste?"

Karmen watched as the girl's mouth dropped open while she put the words together in her mind, folding them over and over again in her brain until they made sense. Then the rage set in and she charged at Karmen with her fists in the air, but Karmen was ready and went at her too. She got the first lick in and kept punching, beating the girl's face in and gnashing her teeth as she pummeled her over and over until she was hit with a punch so forceful it nearly knocked the wind from her lungs.

BLAM!

Karmen toppled over backwards, blinking steadily as she fought to see, but the only thing ahead of her eyes was darkness. Austin kicked at her legs and then jumped on top of her, punching her one more good time before he delivered his instructions.

"Get yo' stupid ass up and go sit in the fuckin' corner!"

Her entire body was sore but the punch hadn't made her stupid. With great difficulty, she rose to her feet and did as he asked. And there she sat the entire night, fuming, as he fucked and snorted lines with girl after girl until the night came to an end.

"Is he still out there?" Austin's voice awoke her, hours later, from a sleep that she didn't even know she'd given in to, and she jumped, blinking hard as she tried to remember where she was. She was still in the club, still sitting by herself in the corner like a child on punishment.

"What da fuck... he didn't go to collect his money from Queen after the job was done?" Austin paused and then the next words out his mouth were ones that Karmen felt would change her current circumstances for the better.

"Gunplay?! Yeah, I heard of that nigga. So he working with him, too? Fuck!"

Gunplay?

Karmen's ears perked up but she knew better than to say a word. Austin ended the call and then she watched as he pointed to one of the girls lying at his feet. Karmen squinted her eyes and noticed it was the same one she'd attacked a few hours before. Although she cleaned up, she still has a small red cut right underneath her eye.

"You comin' with me." After that order, he finally turned and looked at Karmen who was a balled-up mess across the room from where he stood. "Bring ya ass. It's time to go."

The entire ride back to the hotel was awkward as hell to say the least. At least it was for Karmen, who was sitting in the back seat of the Maybach while the random broad up front kept her head in Austin's lap, sucking him off loudly, which Karmen figured was for her benefit. Austin's phone rang and it was the only time the sucking stopped when Austin slapped the girl on the back of the head before ripping her by the hair off of his dick.

"Yo?! You got that info for me, nigga? Takin' yo' ass a long fuckin' time to find dat bitch, J.D."

Karmen's ears perked up as soon as she heard J.D.'s name and she wondered if Lania was found.

"Yessss," Austin hissed, a evil smile crossing his face that told Karmen he'd heard good news. "Kill them all. Her ass, her fuck ass mama and even them fuckin' kids, I don't give a fuck about any of them. Call me when it's finished and you betta not take all day, nigga."

Sucking in a breath, tears came to Karmen's eyes when she heard Austin's orders. She'd wanted Lania dead, yes. But not the babies. She couldn't believe Austin would murder his own children but she was learning not to be surprised about any of the shit a crazy nigga like him would do.

When they got to the hotel, Karmen walked in, ready to go towards the extra bedroom, and close the door behind her on whatever Austin was planning with the woman he'd brought with them. But he had other plans.

"Go clean up while I shower. When I come out, I expect both of y'all to be butt ass naked on the fuckin' bed ready to give daddy some love."

A half-smirk crossed his face and he licked his lips slowly and suggestively, to which the other woman gasped lustfully, but Karmen frowned. If he thought she was about to have a threesome with the same bitch she'd fought, he had another thing coming.

"Hell no!" Karmen barked, unwilling to take any more of his abuse.

It was bad enough she had to put up with the abuse, but now he wanted to humiliate her. She'd finally reached her breaking point and she was going to put her foot down.

"Da fuck you say to me?!"

Boom!

The hit that followed came so fast that Karmen barely had time to prepare herself. Her nose began to squirt blood like a faucet and she flipped backwards, crashing down hard to the tile floor beneath her.

"Clean ya fuckin' face up and do what da fuck I told ya to!"

The next sound she heard as she cradled her nose in her hand was Austin stomping away and the girl's poorly stifled giggles as she laughed at Karmen's expense. After hours of putting on a performance for Austin that she thought would at least grant her immunity from his fists through the night, Austin finally had enough and kicked Karmen out of the room so he could enjoy the stripper chick for himself. And that brought Karmen to the bathroom where she was sitting on the floor with her head in her hands, bawling her heart out and regretting all of the schemes and plots she'd put together to be with Austin in the first place. He was nothing like the man she'd imagined him to be. Lania told her about the abuse, but she made it seem like it was a simple lover's spat they had before fucking the sense out of each other. Karmen now saw that Lania was just as fucked up, if not *more* fucked up, than Austin.

She had to go.

So while Austin continued fucking the stripper senseless, Karmen walked around and packed up every single thing that belonged to her from around the room. She didn't even bother pocketing some of Austin's money or jewelry that he had strewn about their penthouse suite. She didn't want to give him any reason to come looking for her. She'd started from the bottom plenty of times and she was willing to do it again, as long as he would be nowhere around.

Karmen was zipping up the bag and wiping away the last of her fallen tears from her face, when she heard the room door to where Austin was snatch open and slam into the wall with a loud *thump!*

"Where da fuck you think you goin'?"

"I'm leaving," Karmen replied, sniffling, as she squared her shoulders and tried to keep her back straight. It took all the confidence in her to mutter those two words without fear or her knees knocking.

"Leaving, huh?" Austin repeated, and Karmen didn't respond. He seemed oddly calm as he stood in front of her wearing nothing but his birthday suit, his long, thick, and still erect dick pointed towards her.

"Yes, I'm sick of—"

Austin was on her like a ninja before she could finish her sentence. In seconds, he'd grabbed her by the hair, releasing a couple of her tracks from her scalp, along with a few strands of her natural hair, and then reared his arm back, slamming her forcefully against the wall. He knocked her head against it again and again until she was dizzy and her knees went weak. It was only then that he released her and let her fall to the floor.

"The only way you leavin' me is in a body bag," he informed her and then walked away. He slammed the door shut and locked it, knowing that he'd put enough fear in her to keep her from leaving, even though her escape was only feet away.

But he was wrong.

Karmen stayed in place for another hour, waiting until she could hear light snores coming from the room. She then crept out of the door with only her phone in her hand. Normally, Austin's scare tactic would have worked on her, but she now had an ally who probably hated Austin as much as she did in that moment. It provided her with the perfect bargaining tool for her freedom.

Or so she thought.

"Nigga, you look fucked up," was the first thing Gunplay said as soon as he saw Trigga swaggering out that bathroom from taking a shower. "What the hell you been doin'? Wait... don't tell me. Queen got you doin' shit again, huh?"

Limping slightly, Trigga nodded his head. There was no way he could have returned home to Keisha looking the way he had after he'd finished the job Queen had sent him on. She was right in telling him that it wasn't going to be easy because it wasn't. Although Trigga wasn't no stranger to shooting niggas up, he had enough of dealing with the Feds. This would be the second time Queen had sent him on a mission that involved possibly shooting one of them niggas and catching a lifetime bid. The fact that he usually tried to spare their lives made their job easier when it came to taking his.

"She got me on them suicide missions, as usual," Trigga replied back, chuckling a little as he stood in a pair of sweatpants and ran the towel over his chiseled abs, drying them off. Gunplay tossed him a shirt as he puffed hard on a fat blunt.

"Put this shit on, nigga. Don't nobody wanna see yo' fuckin' chest and shit," he joked, and Trigga couldn't help laughing with him.

"So Queen's niggas came by delivering all this hi-tech artillery. I'ma guess that this got somethin' to do with you, and it ain't just her bein' nice to me and breaking me off with some free shit."

"That'll be right," Trigga replied, placing the t-shirt over his head before sitting down on the black leather couch behind him.

Gunplay stood up and walked over to the mini-fridge on the side of the room, and pulled out a Heineken for himself. He waved the bottle in the air to ask Trigga if he wanted one, but closed the door shut when Trigga shook his head. Every man needed a place of peace away from home and away from the trap, and this was Gunplay's. It was a small two-bedroom apartment that he'd bought for himself the moment he stepped out of prison and came up on some funds. He kept it as his getaway whenever LeTavia was tripping or he just needed some time alone. Tonight, it would be the safe house he and Trigga used to plot their next moves.

"I got another text so I'm ready to just go on a search and destroy mission. Last time, I was trying to be patient and wait for shit to fall in place, but I ain't doin' that shit now. Whoever touched my family is here in the city, and I know niggas out here gotta know what's up. I say we run the streets like old times, blasting on muthafuckas until somebody gives us a name."

Placing the bottle to his lips, Gunplay took a sip and then chuckled heavily, shaking his blondish-brown dreads at Trigga's plan.

"So basically, you want to go back to how we did that shit in the old days. I thought you was gon' come in here with some well thought out shit, a diagram with your I's dotted and your T's crossed. Instead, you just want to go on a reckless ass shoot 'em up mission." Gunplay laughed but Trigga didn't join in. He was serious about his plans and ready to get started.

"That's the plan," he said, and Gunplay nodded his head.

"And that's what's up. I'm all in."

Raising the bottle to his lips, Gunplay was about to take a sip when his cell began to ring. He grabbed it and, seeing the number, put it on speaker.

"What you want?"

"I—I need your help. I'm in New York," the woman replied on the other hand. Noting that it was obviously not LeTavia, Trigga narrowed his eyes at Gunplay wondering what was going on. If Gunplay was cheating on LeTavia, it wouldn't be the first time, but it would be the first in a very long time. But it wasn't any of Trigga's business, so he turned his head to give Gunplay his privacy.

"Aye, it ain't like that, B," Gunplay said to Trigga. "This the chick that I know from Dallas. Gave me the info on ya boy."

"Word?" Trigga's eyes widened and his ears tuned in on the call. Whoever was on the other line had his full attention now.

"H—hello?"

"Yeah, I'm here," Gunplay replied. "What da fuck you mean you in New York?"

"He...he found out I was helping you and I had to leave. I need help!"

"Who found out?" Gunplay squinted into the phone. "You mean Austin?"

"Yeah! He found out that I was talking to you... that you asked me about him and he—he beat me. I just landed not too long ago and I just need you to help me get out of the city."

Trigga and Gunplay locked eyes, both of them sure the other one was thinking the same thing. This little informant of Gunplay's, his contact, had assured him that Austin wasn't behind anything that was going on with Trigga. She had said that Austin had been in Dallas the entire time. So if that was true and while someone was snatching Trigga's kids and beating up his wife, Austin was in Texas minding his own damn business, why would he beat her ass for talking to Gunplay? Austin and Gunplay had no issues to speak of. The only answer that made sense was... the bitch was lying.

Gunplay raised the phone to his mouth and spoke in an even tone, although his eyes were seething with his fury. All this fuckin' time had been wasted because this bitch had lied to him. He knew better than to trust someone he used to fuck with and distanced himself from so he could be true to LeTavia, but still, he didn't think she'd try him like that being that she still sent naked photos of herself and flirty messages to his phone from time-to-time.

"Aye, I got you, baby. Just get here. I'll ping you back with the address, a'ight?"

"Oh God, thank you! I'm so sorry, I'm just so scared that he might—"

"Hey, don't be scared about a damn thing. I'ma kill that nigga for real and then you won't have to worry about shit. That's some g-shit right there, you got my word, you good."

As soon as he hung up the phone with her, Gunplay sent off a message to his head of security and told them to load up and head his way. He didn't think that she would be stupid enough to play him for a fool the second time, but he had learned that it could be a deadly mistake to underestimate a woman like Karmen.

21

By the time Gunplay heard the light taps on the door signaling that Karmen had arrived, he and Trigga were strapped and the entire apartment was surrounded by his goons. Fear wasn't something that plagued either one of them, but they'd been in the streets long enough to know that women were often used to set a nigga up. It was one of the oldest tricks in the book, one they'd used themselves plenty times, so they were too smart for it to lead to their own demise.

Gunplay turned to look at Trigga, making sure he was ready for whatever before he opened up the door. Bending his head, Trigga gave him a gentle nod and grazed the top of his pistol with his fingers. His heart was beating in his ears, pumping adrenaline into his veins. He was more than ready to get to the bottom of this situation and so far, this was the first step in the right direction to ending it all. It pissed him off that he'd thought it was Austin to begin with and was now finding out that he'd been right the whole time, but he decided to push all that shit to the side and focus on what he was going to do with whatever they learned.

Opening the door, Gunplay looked out and then stepped to the side without saying a word. Heels clicked on the linoleum floor and when Trigga lifted his eyes, he looked right into the surprised pupils of a woman who appeared to be no more than about twenty-five years old.

Karmen hadn't expected Trigga to be there, but as soon as she saw him, she could see why Lania had been going crazy trying to jump his bones.

Even in her state of panic and fear of Austin retaliating once he realized she'd left, she couldn't help the feeling that erupted between her legs when she looked at the man standing before her.

Jesus.

He was six feet of pure god, covered in tattoos that adorned nearly every bit of his light tan body. His jaw was tight, chiseled and strong, as he pierced her with those beautiful gray eyes. She thought Gunplay was fine, and he was... he was sexy as fuck. But *this* man? She had lost all her words. That is, until Gunplay nudged her in her side.

"Sit down and tell me what happened."

Karmen did as he asked, noting that they didn't follow suit and continued to stand over her, hovering and making her feel as if she had walked into a police interrogation room. She swallowed the lump in her throat and forced herself to ramble through her well-rehearsed lie.

"Austin is after me... he wants to kill me because he found out that you called and asked about him, but that I told you he was—"

"But why the fuck would that nigga want to kill you because you talked to me?" Gunplay questioned impatiently. It was obvious that she was sticking to the same bullshit lie so he decided to get right to it.

"Um, he—"

"Me and Austin ain't never had no shit between us. So it must be somethin' you hidin'. Was that nigga really in Texas the whole time like you said?"

Gunplay's tone was aggressive and beads of sweat rose up on Karmen's forehead before spotting her entire face in a matter of seconds. Her eyes darted to the left and she suddenly realized it may have been a mistake for her to come here. She'd been desperate and in her desperation, hadn't carefully thought out her plan of escape. Instead, her actions had led her from one lion's den into another. And this current lion's den was likely more dangerous than the first.

"He—no, he wasn't in Texas the entire time," she admitted, licking her lips with a tongue that felt like she'd ran it back and forth over sandpaper. "I lied because h—he gave me money to lie."

"So you tryin' to say he knew I was gon' call? Or that you ran your mouth to him as soon as I did? What—you his girl or somethin'?"

Karmen shook her head and then jumped when Gunplay took out his gun and released the safety before placing it in his lap. Her eyes went to it and then filled up with tears the moment her brain registered that this could all end the opposite from how she'd fantasized it. She glanced over to Trigga for... for what? For help? Comfort? Mercy? Either way, none of that was in his cool gray eyes that were blistering with the same emotion that Gunplay had in his: pure hate and murderous intent.

"No, I'm not... I mean, I was, but I left him and..."

"You left him and now you comin' to me to give you some protection?" Gunplay finished for her. A lone tear fell down her cheek and she flicked it away while nodding her head.

In one quick motion, Gunplay picked up the gun and held it up, pressing the barrel into her forehead so hard that it broke skin, and droplets of blood began sliding down her face, mixing with her tears as she shrieked in pain.

"Speak! Where is he?"

Karmen was a lot of things but a thug she was not. And although she'd played with the idea of being Austin's ride or die, she'd never firmly committed to the role, so it didn't take much more to have her singing like a prized songbird.

"H—he's staying in the penthouse at the W Hotel! We just flew in a couple days ago!"

Gunplay looked over at Trigga who was already five steps ahead of him, rooting through Karmen's bag to back up her story. He saw a keycard for the suite at the W but it still wasn't enough. Turning it around, he dialed the number and put the phone to her mouth after placing it on speaker. Karmen already knew what he wanted so she didn't need any additional instruction.

"Hello, this is Karmen... I just left there. Um... I'm staying in the penthouse suite."

And I'm the one who just walked out of there bloody and with a black eye, she stopped herself from adding.

"Oh, yes, I remember. Do—do you need anything brought up to the room for your return?" the clerk asked, before adding in a low whisper, "Or do you need me to call the authorities for you?"

"No, no, that's okay. I just wanted to know if you could tell me if Austin left out already or whether he's still there."

The woman replied, still whispering through the line. "Um, yes, he's still up there with that...*other* woman. If you need anything, just let me know and I can help. I saw... I saw your eye."

Before Karmen could say another word, the cell was pulled away from her lips and the call was ended.

"What is he planning?"

That question came from Trigga who had pulled out his own weapon and was pressing it firmly into her cheek, making a dimple right in the space he envisioned his bullet piercing.

"I—I don't know! He hasn't told anyone his plan. I just know that the nigga you killed last night... the one Queen sent you after, he set that up! It was part of his plan."

That threw Trigga for a loop, and even Gunplay had to think again about what she was saying. Was Karmen suggesting that Austin was working with Queen?

"Da fuck you mean by that?!" Gunplay shouted, pressing his gun harder into her head.

"Th—the guy was doing side deals with Austin, but Austin knew he was working with Queen but too far down on the totem pole for him to really be an asset to him. So he set him up, got him in trouble with the FBI because he knew the nigga would start talking and demanding protective custody. He knew that Queen would only trust Trigga to kill him. I—I—I don't know why, but he wanted that to happen. He wanted Trigga to be working back with Queen!"

Gunplay and Trigga exchanged glances but neither one knew why Austin would want Trigga to pair up with Queen. An alliance with Queen meant that Trigga would have the backing to annihilate Austin with ease if she was backing him. How was that part of his plan?

"What else you know? Speak!"

"Th—that's it, I promise! He didn't tell me much, I haven't even been fuckin' with him that long. I—"

The kill shot came quick. And so did the satisfaction Trigga felt when he saw the wall behind her splatter with blood and brain matter before her body dropped to the ground. For several seconds, he and Gunplay sat there, thinking to themselves about what they'd just learned, and then both of them simultaneously started making moves. Gunplay, to make a call to his clean up squad who would remove Karmen's dead body and, Trigga, to change out the newly bloodied clothes so they could go pay Austin a visit.

In less than thirty minutes, Trigga and Gunplay were at the W with a team of Gunplay's most trusted and skilled soldiers with them, standing in Austin's empty penthouse suite. He was gone. Initially, they thought all was lost until they were about to leave and noticed that the hotel had slid a one page piece of paper under the door. It was the bill.

Interestingly enough, the bill wasn't made out to Austin but to another man by the name of Ozell Jenkins who had a Brooklyn address.

"Find him," Gunplay ordered one of his men, and the guy wasted no time pulling out his cell phone to follow the instructions he was given. When they walked out of the hotel, the sun was rising on a brand-new day.

Trigga looked at his watch and shot Keisha a text to let her know he was good so that she wouldn't worry about him being gone for so long. When he lifted his head, Gunplay had his phone in his hand, texting as well. Trigga figured he was probably doing the same thing: letting LeTavia know that he'd be missing for a little longer.

"I hope you ain't tired after whatever shit Queen had you in last night," Gunplay said, tucking his phone in his back pocket. "It looks like we 'bout to have a long fuckin' day."

22

"So both of us are on our own again tonight, huh?" LeTavia asked, plopping her ass down on Keisha's sofa as she tossed a handful of freshly popped popcorn into her mouth. "Just like the old days. Them niggas in the streets, and you and me left to watch chick flicks until we fall the fuck out."

Smiling, Keisha nodded her head and hummed in agreement as she stuffed her own mouth with the buttery, warm popcorn. It had nearly been a full twenty-four hours since she'd seen Trigga, and she was trying not to panic but it didn't feel right. He was so secretive these days and she hated it. She knew that he was never a man of many words, and she also knew that he didn't tell her what he was up to for fear that it would worry her to death. But she also knew that all of these things left him with the perfect opportunity to be unfaithful.

And she couldn't push away the nagging feeling in her mind that this wasn't a new feeling. She couldn't remember much from the moments that she'd lost after being attacked, but she did feel like she'd been convinced for some reason that Trigga had been cheating on her with some chick at the club. Now after speaking with Lania, and hearing about him leaving with Toy, who Keisha still couldn't get in contact with, it seemed like she may have been on to something.

"Hopefully, they won't be gone too long," Keisha replied, and LeTavia scoffed before rolling her eyes.

"I can take a break from Gunplay. We're not all up each other's ass like how you and Trigga are," she teased in her normal rude way, but Keisha only smirked at her and nudged her gently with her shoulder.

"It's called 'love,' Tavi. You so fuckin' rude."

LeTavia laughed and pushed more popcorn between her lips. "Shit, I love my nigga too, but I can't say I don't enjoy having some time alone every now and then so that I can spend by myself or with my girls. You don't like that?"

Pushing her lips together, Keisha's eyes rose to the ceiling as she mulled the thought over in her mind. Long after she'd already settled on her response, she finally shook her head. No, she never wanted or needed to be apart from Trigga. In fact, when he wasn't around, all she wanted was for him to be with her. She could go her entire life and not have time alone and be perfectly fine. Deep down, she hoped that he loved her company just as much as she enjoyed his.

"Humph. Y'all weird," was Letavia's response, and then they both fell out laughing at the same moment that the doorbell rang.

Jumping up, Keisha wiped her greasy fingertips on her sweats and then walked to the door, initially not thinking to check the peephole, but then she thought twice and glanced through it to be sure. Queen's men were stationed all outside, but even still, she knew it was smart to be safe rather than sorry. After seeing Rodney, one of Queen's top security members, standing in front of the door, she unlocked it.

"Hey, sorry to bother you, but we got a..." He paused and pulled up a transmitter of some sort from by his side. "What's the chick name again?"

"LUH-NEE—UH!" Lania's voice came through the speaker, revealing every bit of her agitation of being hemmed up in front of Keisha's house like the untrustworthy thot she actually was. "And I don't appreciate being treated like this. Me and Keisha are good friends, so I don't know why y'all actin' like you ain't never—"

Rodney cut down the sound and looked at Keisha, waiting for her order.

"You can let her in," Keisha replied with a roll of her eyes. Rodney twisted his lips up a little, glanced to the side, and then looked back at Keisha.

"Well, she wouldn't give us her social security number so we couldn't run a quick background check. Without that, I'm not sure we should—"

"You can let her in," Keisha repeated. "She works at Trigga's club and I spoke to her the last time I was there. She's fine."

Keisha waited by the door until she saw Lania being escorted to it by two men who were at either side of her. The sour expression on Lania's face told her that she wasn't the least bit pleased with the level of security that she'd had to go through in order to get inside, but as soon as her eyes fell on Keisha, her lips curled into a genuine smile.

"Heyyy, girrrrrll!"

Lania ran up and wrapped her arms around Keisha's neck, hugging her tightly. Keisha returned the embrace, forcing herself to remember that this woman was supposedly her friend. But their bond didn't seem genuine at all. She wanted to ask Trigga about this new so-called friend she'd gained, but with him being away, she hadn't been offered the opportunity.

"What are you doing here?" Keisha asked, pulling away from the hug.

"Keesh! Oh God! You forgot about our Wednesday girl-time dates!" Lania said with a roll of her eyes. "How could you forget? It was your idea to start it!"

"Mm hmm," Keisha mumbled, wondering when she'd ever been the type of woman to have a weekly movie time meeting with *anyone*. She was not the pajama party type and definitely wasn't a girly girl to be planning a girl's time date.

"Who is this?" LeTavia asked as soon as they walked in the living room. Keisha stuffed her hands in her pockets and gave a gentle shrug before replying.

"This is Lania... my friend from the club."

"Your *friend?*" LeTavia echoed, looking Lania up and down with skepticism. "Since when? I mean... I know I haven't talked to you in a minute because I was out of town, and then there was the accident, but I wasn't gone that damn long."

She regarded Lania with her nose turned up as if she stunk, and Lania immediately knew that she was going to have a hard time getting to Keisha with her long-necked, modelesque looking friend hanging around.

"We are new friends. I started working at the club only a few weeks before Keisha's accident."

"Oh, so you mean during the time that Keisha can't recall?" LeTavia further clarified. "You became Keisha's friend around the time that she can't remember. So basically... she can't remember being your friend, you simply informed her that y'all are close, huh?"

"Well...yeah," Lania replied and shot Keisha a look as if to ask what was wrong with LeTavia. Unbeknownst to Keisha, LeTavia had every reason to be suspicious.

"I mean, to be honest, I've never heard of you either. Keisha has never spoke about you so I guess we're in the same boat, huh?" Lania beamed, even though she knew that her words were said with a little bite. "What's your name anyways?"

"No, heffa, we aren't in the same boat because unlike your ass, Keisha remembers me. You probably never heard of me because yo' fake ass ain't—"

"Whoa, Tavi! Hold on a minute," Keisha cut in, walking in the middle of the two women to separate them.

"Keesh, I don't trust her ass," LeTavia hissed, keeping her eyes on Lania who was smiling smugly behind Keisha's back.

"Lania... can you give us a minute to talk? Tavi, walk with me into the kitchen to get the drinks ready, please."

"Sure!" Lania replied with ease. She knew that out of the two of them, LeTavia was the only one who seemed crazy in that moment. She hadn't done a thing but walked in and been attacked. Surely, Keisha wouldn't let someone just jump on one of her friends like that.

"I have to use the bathroom anyways. Um... where is—"

"If you was a real fuckin' friend, you wouldn't have to ask!" LeTavia shot out, catching Lania before she had a chance to notice that she'd slipped. Keisha caught it too and made a note of the fact that Lania swore they had these 'girl pow-wow' meetings all the time but was about to ask where the bathroom was.

"No, I know where it is!" Lania chirped, a little too pleasantly. "It's just been so long. You know, with Keisha's accident and all."

Keisha pulled LeTavia to the kitchen and Lania pretended to go to the bathroom, but bypassed it and went straight into the master bedroom that was at the end of the hall. Walking in, she ran the tips of her fingers along the edge of the bed, closing her eyes and biting down hard on her bottom lip as she thought about how this was the same exact bed that Trigga laid his body in. The same bed that he fucked his wife in now, but soon, and very, *very* soon, it would be the one he'd fuck her in.

Leaning down, she pressed her nose into one of the pillows, knowing that it was the one he laid his head on when she smelled his cologne. She kissed it gently after taking several deep breaths of his fragrance and then, just as she was about to move on to something else, another thought occurred to her. A devious one at that. Lifting her short mini dress, she slipped off the pink lace thong from her ass, parted her legs and grabbed the pillow.

Closing her eyes, she opened her legs and pushed the pillow up into her folds, dampening it with her juices as she humped it shamelessly, quickly bringing herself to an orgasm as she thought about Trigga. On the foot of the bed was one of his shirts, and she grabbed it with one hand, draped it across her face, and then breathed deeply, taking in his scent as she continued rocking her hips over his pillow, bringing herself to ecstasy. She came in a matter of seconds and then spent a few seconds more enjoying the waves of euphoria that fell on her. She could still hear Keisha and LeTavia arguing in the kitchen, but she couldn't care less about what they were saying. Her mind was full of nothing but Trigga.

After wiping her juices with his pillow, she tucked it back onto the top of the bed, smiling gently at the idea of him falling asleep to her sweet scent, and then continued around the room, touching all of his things. After a few moments more, she decided to leave, telling herself that this would be her room soon enough. But she had to be patient. She couldn't get caught.

Walking out, she was just about to head into the bathroom to freshen up when another room caught her eye. She looked inside and saw that it was none other than the other person who would occupy Trigga's heart along with her, once she was able to get rid of Keisha. She couldn't resist walking into the room and over to the child's bedside, wondering how much he looked like his father. The day Austin kidnapped him, she hadn't been with him because she was spending time at the club with Trigga. She had no idea what Trigga's son looked like.

But upon first glance, she saw that he was the spitting image of his father. Leaning down, she closed her eyes and kissed him gently on his forehead. He stirred slightly and then opened his mouth and whispered...

"Mama?"

"Yes, baby, it's me," Lania replied, whispering against his forehead. Cameron smiled lightly and still in the midst of sleep, snuggled back into the covers and in seconds was back in his deep sleep.

"Keesh, all I'm sayin' is that you may need to get some hypnosis or some shit to bring back ya fuckin' memory because anyone can see that this bitch is foul! Somethin' ain't right with her!"

Not saying anything, Keisha sat down on top of one of her barstools, feeling pressure that she wasn't sure she was ready for. On one hand, she didn't want to take LeTavia's warnings lightly. But on the other hand, why would Lania lie about being her friend? What did she have to gain?

"I really can't remember, Tavi! And the things that she said about her miscarriage and all... how I helped her out so she could take care of her kids. That stuff sounds like me. It's something I would do!"

LeTavia scoffed and rolled her eyes for the millionth time since Lania had showed up.

"That ain't no hard shit to come up with! Anyone with a mind knows that kids are a soft spot to a mother. See, that shit wouldn't have worked on me because I don't have kids and I don't trust nan bitch around my man. But word travels fast around a strip club, so I'm sure most of them in there knew about what happened to Sade and they know you'd give your life for Cam. Now you can do what you want, but I wouldn't trust that bitch to be all up in my personal life. Bad enough her hoe ass workin' with your man."

As soon as LeTavia finished what she was saying, Lania walked in from the hallway, her eyes pulled tight and narrowed in on LeTavia's face.

"You know what? I'm goin' to go ahead and leave. I have some things I need to do and I think it's a bit too crowded in here for me to stay."

Neither Keisha nor LeTavia moved to change her mind. But instead of shooting her daggers of hate through her eyes as LeTavia was, Keisha stood up to walk her out, gently wrapping her arm around her shoulders.

"You have to excuse LeTavia. She's just worried about me, that's all. She's a great friend once you get to know her."

"Her ass won't get to know shit about me," LeTavia huffed from behind them, but Keisha continued walking Lania to the door, ignoring her.

"I can't take you nowhere! Damn, you so rude," Keisha said to LeTavia once Lania was out the door.

"I rather be rude than stupid," she replied back, cutting her eyes at Keisha, who was instantly offended by her statement. "And stupid is what you'll be if you keep believing that shit ole girl is saying. We were just talkin' about how you always in Trigga's ass. Does it even make sense that you would plan some weekly movie date shit with her during the time when Trigga would normally be home or resting so he could get to work? That bitch is bogus!"

Long after LeTavia left, Trigga still wasn't home and Keisha couldn't get to sleep. For one, she couldn't get over feeling angry about not being able to make herself remember things that she'd forgotten. And secondly, for some reason, her bed smelled like ass.

"Ugh!" Keisha groaned, finally decided that she needed to just change the sheet and start a load of laundry since sleep was out of the equation.

She wanted Trigga home, but her only real solace was knowing that wherever he was, he was with Gunplay and not another bitch. At least she

knew that this time when he said he was working, she knew that was definitely what he was doing. Keisha snatched the sheets and pillowcases off the
bed and then after another whiff of the pillows, wrinkled up her nose and
decided to dump them in there as well.

When she loaded the washer, she realized there was more than enough
room left to toss in the clothes that Trigga had worn that week and thrown
on the floor. He was a true man. He could be standing on top of a dirty
clothes hamper and still would drop his dirty clothes right on the floor or
pitch them over the foot of the bed. Grabbing the shirt that he'd taken off
the day before and placed across the end of their bed, Keisha paused when
she saw something reddish near the collar.

"Is that lipstick?"

She squinted at the spot on the shirt and then held it up to the light.

"No... it can't be," she told herself and lobbed it in the basket by her side.

Grabbing up a few more of Trigga's things, she put them in the basket
and then hauled it to the laundry room to load everything inside of the
washer. After flinging in his socks, boxers, and shirts, Keisha started on his
jeans, checking his pockets before placing them inside, since Trigga had a
habit of leaving change and all kinds of other things in his pockets. But
when she reached into a pair of jeans that he'd worn a couple days back, the
same day as the shirt with the red mark, she reached in and pulled out a
light pink, lace thong.

"Oh my God, Trigga... what did you do?!"

23

It was the next day by the time Trigga came home, tired as fuck and barely able to stand on his own two feet. His anger and need for revenge told him he needed to continue on, but his body gave up on him and shut down. He'd been up on his killing mission for over forty-eight hours straight, and he couldn't even trust himself to shoot straight. His mind was playing tricks on him. He was delirious, but it could be solved with a good rest and then he'd be at it again.

"Daddy!!!!" Cameron shot out of his chair at the kitchen table and ran over to Trigga, hugging him so tightly and with so much force that he nearly toppled over.

"Hey, lil' man! What's up?" Trigga greeted his son, using almost the last of his strength. "Where's ya mama?"

"In the room," Cameron replied and just that quick, the show playing on television had stolen his attention.

He pulled away from Trigga and sat back down at the table, pushing spoonfuls of cereal in his mouth with his eyes glued on the screen. Normally, Trigga would have fought against Cameron eating and watching TV at the same time, but he didn't have the mental wherewithal to put up a fight.

Walking into the room, he was barely able to make it into the door before Keisha jumped up in front of his face, dangling a pink, lace thong from her forefinger. Trigga backed away and wrinkled up his nose, trying to wrap his mind around the image in front of him and decipher why Keisha seemed so pissed to be holding up her own damn panties.

"What da fuck, Keesh?!"

"'What da fuck, is what I should be sayin' to you!"

Reaching out, she mushed him on the side of the head and though Keisha's strength was no match for his, the fact that he was so fatigued worked in her favor and he fell back against the door, pushing it closed with his body.

"Whose fuckin' thong is this, Maurice?"

"I don't fuckin' know!" Trigga replied back with more roughness in his tone than he would have had he been in his right mind. "Get dat shit out my fuckin' face. I'm tired as fuck. Too fuckin' tired to play these games with your ass."

Keisha's neck snapped back and she gave him an incredulous look, not believing that he was the one with the thong in his pants but wanted to act like she was in the wrong.

"Games?! Trigga, I found these thongs in your jeans. The ones you were wearing the other night. And they are *not* mine so don't even go there!"

"How da fuck you know?!" Trigga roared so loud that Keisha jumped back several paces, almost stumbling over her own feet. "How do you fuckin' know them ain't yo' fuckin' panties, Keesh?! You don't know shit else! Couldn't tell me who da fuck attacked you or no shit like that, but you can tell me about some greasy ass thongs you found in my jeans? Get da fuck outta here with that bullshit." Trigga fanned her away and Keisha's jaw dropped open as tears filled her eyes.

"But Lania told me that she saw you and Toy leaving together and—"

"Lania?! I don't' give a fuck what that bitch—listen, I'm tired as fuck. I been in the streets tryin' to find a nigga who beat your ass... I've been bodying niggas all night behind *you* and you wanna question me about a *thong*? I'm about to take my tired ass to sleep and when I wake up, I don't wanna hear shit about no other bitch, because ain't no bitch in my life right now but you!"

Both of them knew that when Trigga woke up and was in his right state of mind, he'd regret those words, but that realization didn't make them hurt Keisha any less. Picking her mouth up from the floor, she turned away as Trigga stripped down and got under the covers and walked out of the room, closing the door behind her.

The atmosphere around him seemed like it could have been taken straight from out of an Alfred Hitchcock movie. It looked as if it should have been pouring down raining outside; the clouds were gray and the air was humid. Every now and then, a bolt of lightning would illuminate the skies, making Austin think of the old adage that 'the devil was beating his wife.' There was a stench in the air that reminded him of the day he dropped his first body, a nigga by the name of Semaj, who he killed before dumping his body mercilessly in a dumpster. Semaj's crime? He'd stolen money that Austin had saved up all summer. It wasn't much, only about sixty dollars in total, but to Austin, it was all about principle. He wanted niggas to know that you couldn't fuck with what was his and get away with it.

Years ago, Trigga had stolen from Austin. Not directly, he'd actually stolen from Lloyd, but once Austin took over Lloyd's empire, the loss fell under him. When Trigga refused to return the money, Austin let it go because he had other shit occupying his time. His empire was growing daily to the point that he had to have his attention on it at all times. His niggas in Texas already knew the deal; he wasn't a weak nigga and wasn't to be tested. But it took a little time and gun power to convince the ones in his new territories. Now everything was running smoothly for him, but he had his eyes on a bigger prize... which led him back to Trigga. Not only was he going to pay for the money he'd stolen, but he was the means to an even greater end. He was the key to getting to Queen.

Unfortunately for Austin, he knew the only way to get over on Trigga was to use the element of surprise to his advantage and—judging from the two bodies lying at his feet—he'd lost that.

"Fuck!" Austin cursed as he peered at the iPad screen in front of him and looked at the mutilated bodies of Karmen as well as his nigga, Ozell.

While Karmen's was a simple death, a single shot through to the dome, it was obvious that Ozell had severely suffered through the use of multiple torture tactics used to extract information. He was missing fingers and toes, his head was covered with lesions from being smashed multiple times with the butt of a gun, and every single tooth at the front of his mouth was missing. On the wall behind him, written in his crimson red blood was the word 'Austin,' with the picture of duel pistols, a symbol that both Trigga and Gunplay had adopted. He'd been discovered and it was all thanks to that bitch, Karmen.

"FUCK!" Austin screamed, punching his hand into the wall beside him. He wished he'd never laid eyes on Karmen in the first place.

She had betrayed him and still lost her life. What a stupid bitch. She was nothing like Lania, and Austin almost regretted telling J.D. to kill her. Lania had rode by his side for years, through tons of shit and hundreds of women. She was just as crazy as he was and that's why it worked. No matter how much she tried to convince herself that she wanted a different life for herself and her kids, Austin knew the truth. She was his perfect match—they belonged together. Or at least they did until she betrayed him for Trigga. So she had to die, but it was okay; Austin would find a replacement. Obviously, Karmen wasn't it.

"What you want us to do, boss?"

Austin took a final look at both of the bodies in front of him and then waved his hand as he turned away and pushed the iPad to the side, simultaneously ending the video.

"Wrap 'em up and dump 'em. I don't want this shit coming back to me. Clean my fuckin' name up off the wall."

Standing out on the balcony of his new suite at the Ritz, Austin turned to Mendozo, one of his top men who had accompanied him from Dallas to New York, and decided to inform him of his change in plans. There was no more need to lay low anymore because Trigga already knew who was after him. And this was *Trigga's* city, meaning that they didn't have long before they were found if they kept taking things slow, waiting for Austin's carefully thought out plan to eventually unfold. There was no time for that anymore, so he had to take matters in his own hands. He had to get to Trigga before he found him first.

"I don't want no fuckin' body laying their heads down on a goddamn pillow until y'all find this nigga. He's cocky... he won't be too hard to find because I guarantee you, he won't be hiding. Station someone at all of his usual spots and call me when you got eyes on that nigga."

"You'll hear from me soon," Mendozo replied before turning away and placing two fingers in his mouth, whistling loudly to signal all the other men sitting in the living room of the suite so that he could share Austin's orders.

As much as Austin believed himself to be fearless, now that Trigga knew he was behind it all, he wasn't as calm and collected as he appeared to be. He'd increased his security detail and even sent word back home for them to fire up the jet and send more of his crew to the city. One thing he did not do was underestimate Trigga. That was the mistake that his cousin, Lloyd, had made, and he paid for it with his life.

24

*B*y the time Trigga awoke, Keisha was gone. The first thing he did was grab his phone and dial her number. He remembered the things he'd said to her and, like he knew he would, he regretted every word. He'd been exhausted, mentally drained, and hungry. Although the words he said felt true at the time, he'd said them in anger and he didn't mean for them to come out that way.

He didn't mean to voice his frustrations so roughly to her because he knew Keisha better than anyone in the world, and no matter how strong she appeared to be, she was a gentle, soft, and caring person on the inside. And she lived off of every word that Trigga said. He was her husband and could change her whole world by the uttering of a few words. He could determine her mood, calm her mind, uplift her spirits, all by what came out of his mouth. Trigga didn't need anyone to tell him that he'd crushed her, and all he could hope was that she hadn't left him again.

Keisha didn't answer his call and he felt his heart thump in his chest as he stood, trying to swallow down the panic that took over his body. It wasn't until he began to walk towards his bedroom door that he heard voices coming from the living room.

"You *must* concentrate, Cameron!"

"But I want to go back to school with my friends," Cameron whined. When Trigga peeked around the corner, he saw Cameron was stubbornly poking out his lip in protest.

"You can't go back to school with your friends right now, Cam. Your parents want you to be homeschooled for now. Maybe soon that will change, but until then, you have to concentrate on your studies. You don't want to have to do all this over again, do you?"

Trigga sat back and watched as his son thought about his teacher's question for a minute, before gently shaking his head 'no.'

"No, Mrs. Ce-Ce."

"I didn't think so. Now finish this sheet and we can move on to the next one," Mrs. Ce-Ce replied, and sighed deeply in relief when she saw Cameron pick up his pencil to continue his work. He was a great kid, but she couldn't lie and say that he didn't make her earn every penny his parents paid for him to be homeschooled. He was stubborn to a fault and unapologetically so.

"Hey, Mrs. Ce-Ce, what's happenin'?" Trigga greeted the older woman, barely looking her in her eyes as he pecked on his phone. He was sending a message to Gunplay to let him know that he was juiced up and ready to go.

"Oh nothing. We're going to have a great day today." She looked at Cameron and gave him a pointed look. "Right, Cameron?"

Cameron responded by wrinkling up his nose in protest, but still answered accordingly.

"Yes, Mrs. Ce-Ce."

Trigga couldn't help but chuckle a little at his son's antics. And then in the next second, his mind was on Keisha once again.

"Did Keisha say when she would be back?"

Mrs. Ce-Ce shook her head while instructing Cameron with a pointed finger to continue his work. He groaned but obeyed.

"No, she didn't say when she would be back. Just that she was going to her kickboxing class and would return once it was over."

That somewhat calmed Trigga's spirits, so he retreated back into the room to shower and get ready to get back on the job. It wasn't until he was stepping out of the shower that he happened to look down in the small trash can near the toilet, while he was drying off, and focused on the pink lace thong inside; the same one that Keisha had been holding when she questioned him about another woman. He froze in place, thinking through the things she'd said, and then cursed aloud when something occurred to him.

He didn't give a damn about Keisha finding no thong because he was still convinced it was hers and she simply couldn't remember. That was the only explanation, being that he'd never done anything with any other woman that would cause him to end up with her thong in his pocket. What stunned him was the fact that Keisha had brought up Lania's name.

But Lania told me that she saw you and Toy leaving together and—

Keisha hadn't finished her sentence before Trigga interrupted, but he didn't need to know what else she needed to say. The bottom line was that Lania had told her something that had her questioning him. Something concerning him leaving with Toy, a woman he hadn't seen since before Keisha was attacked. How did she even talk to Keisha? When did she get the chance?

Trigga didn't know what kind of games she was playing, but he knew that he was going to have to find out. Sooner rather than later.

"Where you at?" Trigga asked with an even tone as he strode through the city in slow-mo as if he had nowhere to go.

Truthfully, he had a million things to take care of and he would be on top of it as soon as he caught up with Lania to see why she was fuckin' with his family. Trigga hadn't survived the streets for so long because he ignored his instincts. His instincts were what had kept him alive for so long; he trusted them and they never steered him wrong. Everything in him was saying that something was up with Lania.

"I'm at the club, duh!" She giggled, twirling a lock of her hair around her finger as she spoke. "Why? You comin' to see me?"

It had been more than a few days since she'd seen Trigga, and sitting around his office, touching everything he left in it, and smelling his chair was no longer cutting it. She was tired of looking at his pictures and pretending he was there with her in the room as she massaged her clit and imagined it was his rock-hard dick. She wanted him to be there in the flesh.

"Yeah," was all he said and then the line went dead.

Frowning into the phone, Lania wondered what was the cause for his abruptness but quickly shook that away and reminded herself that he was on the way to see her in a few so there was no need to pout. She removed her wet fingers from out of her panties, where she'd lodged them the moment that she heard Trigga's voice, and patted her throbbing clit with her hand.

"Just hold out for the real thing. Daddy's coming," she whispered before sucking her own juices from her fingertips and sneaking out of Trigga's office.

She was in the locker room picking out her outfits for the night, when she heard the sound of heavy footsteps from behind her and whirled around, her heavy bosoms bouncing around ahead of her as she stood stark naked in front of Trigga.

"Oh! I was just about to change!" Lania said truthfully.

She had been about to change but what she had chosen to put on was barely more than the naked body she presently had on display. Trigga's facial expression was tight and his eyes were piercing and sharp, but he didn't even flinch to indicate whether or not he'd heard what she'd said or whether he was even the least bit affected by her standing before him in the nude.

"What did you tell my wife?"

"Huh?" Lania asked, her brows bunched tightly in confusion.

"My wife... Keisha. What did you tell her about me and Toy?" he questioned, taking a step closer.

"I didn't—I..."

Lania's eyes darted around as she tried to come up with a believable lie that would knock Trigga off her trail. She should have known that Keisha was the type to run back and tell her man everything like an idiot. You were supposed to wait until you had proof before you questioned a man about a woman. *Solid* proof. But of course, Keisha wouldn't know that. She went blabbing everything she'd heard the first chance she got.

The entire room was so quiet that the only sound that could be heard came from the A.C. running through the vents. Trigga stared at Lania through the slits of his eyes, wondering if he would actually have to kill Lania. He was on a mission to protect his family at all costs and he didn't have the patience to deal with anyone who threatened that.

"Da fuck? Do I gotta ask you the same shit again?!"

Lania jumped at the tone of his voice but still didn't speak. She pushed backwards until her back thumped against the locker behind her and wrapped her arms around her body as her bottom lip began to quiver. What could she tell him?

"Fuck it," Trigga said finally and she closed her eyes tightly, letting out a yelp when she saw him move as if going for a gun.

"It was Queen!" she cried, freezing Trigga in place.

Queen?! he thought, his mind blown. How the hell did Lania know Queen in the first place? And what did she have to do with this situation?

"The fuck are you talkin' 'bout? How do you know Queen?"

With her eyes wide, Lania spewed the rest of her story making sure to skip parts that would have made her look bad. She was an expert at making herself the victim and she hoped that it would work once again.

"S—she came to me one day while I was here. I was desperate! She told me that you were her best hitta and she needed you back because you bein' gone was bad for business. She told me that Keisha was the only reason that you refused to work with her so she asked me to shake shit up between you two—"

"What the *fuck*?!" Trigga roared.

"I—I didn't do anything that she asked except tell Keisha that you were with Toy after she came to the club asking where you were. I guess you'd been gone all night and—"

Bam!

Bam!

Bam!

Turning around, Trigga started smashing his fist into one of the lockers near him over and over again until his knuckles got red and started to bleed. *This* was the fucked up part of being out of the game. It was a fucked up hustle because the foundation of it all was selfishness. It was impossible to be anything but selfish because, in the streets, the strong preyed on the weak. To find someone's weakness and exploit that to benefit your own greed, those were the rules and it was what had once made Trigga such a successful killer. It was what made Queen such a successful queenpin. He just never for once thought that she would turn the shit on him. But the other rule of the streets was that once you were in, you couldn't get out. He'd broken that rule and here were the consequences.

There was one more thing that Trigga had to know. Queen's name was coming up more than he wanted it to and he was going to get to the bottom of it. First, the chick Karmen had said that Austin's plan revolved around him working with Queen. Now, Lania was telling him that Queen had encouraged her to fuck up his marriage so that he could work with her as well. If he found out that Queen was also the one helping Austin bleed him for money... if she had *anything* to do with Keisha being attacked, there was no way in hell he could let that slide.

"The photo you saw of my wife kissing another man. Was Queen behind that?"

The color drained from Lania's face before she could answer and when Trigga saw it, he already knew the truth. He covered his face with his hands and gritted his teeth together so hard the enamel began to screech.

"I can't fuckin' believe this shit."

"Yes, but I don't really know because—"

"Listen. You need to be really sure about this because the same envelope that had that photo in it is the one that I found after the nigga who shot up my club and laid his hands on my fuckin' wife gave me an address to meet him at. So think hard and tell me if you know for *sure* whether or not Queen was behind that."

"Well..."

Lania stopped speaking when she realized that she was about to implicate herself as being involved with Austin. The truth was Queen had given her an envelope the day she spoke with her for the first time and told her not to look in it. She'd instructed her to leave it on Trigga's desk one day when he wasn't around. She ended up taking the envelope home after being unsuccessful with delivering it and when she looked for it again, it was gone.

Austin had taken it assuming that she was doing her part to help him and she never told him otherwise because both parties that she was taking orders from were happy on her end. Austin was satisfied that he was on her team, going above and beyond to help him fuck with Trigga's mind, and once she told Queen that her package had been delivered to Trigga, she deposited money in Lania's account to show her gratitude in her own special way. It was a win across the board. But how could she explain that to Trigga? She couldn't.

"No, I don't think that she was behind that. All I know is what I told you already."

For several seconds, Trigga just stared into her analyzing every bit of her for any hint of dishonesty. Lania squirmed under his gaze until he finally released her and turned away. The moment she heard him walk out the door, slamming it behind him, she sunk to her knees and cried. Her heart was breaking as she realized she probably fucked her chances with Trigga for good.

25

"Aye, Trigga, what's happenin', nigga?" one of Queen's security members greeted Trigga with a smile before walking over to pat him down.

The benefit of being a close friend of Queen's was that he knew where she laid her head, which was a privilege denied by many and only earned after years and years of one proving their loyalty to her. But regardless of any history shared, everybody got patted down before they saw the Queen. It didn't matter who you were, if you weren't Queen or her immediate family, you had to go through security.

"Ain't shit happenin', man. How's business been?"

The man chuckled, shaking his head as he finished searching Trigga for weapons. "You know we ain't never slowing down over here. But I can't complain."

"And you never will," Trigga replied, still trying to play it cool. Inside, he was burning with anger, but he knew better than to think that he'd really be able to touch Queen the way he would a nigga on the streets. Thinking back, he realized that for the last couple months, since Lania started working at the club, he'd never been allowed to see Queen in private. Every single time he spoke to her in person, her husband Dre was around. Although it struck him as odd, Trigga never thought much about it until now. He realized that Dre was aware that his wife was up to some foul shit, and his presence was there to protect her in case Trigga happened to find out.

"Fuckin' bitch," Trigga muttered under his breath.

"What was that?"

The man finished searching Trigga and stood back, his eyes narrowed as he watched his face carefully.

"Nothing. Was thinking 'bout some shit that happened down at the club," Trigga lied with ease, not even flinching.

But still, Queen's security wasn't top of the line for nothing. The man continued to keep his eyes on Trigga even after he beckoned him to go ahead and walk inside. Once Trigga was down the hall, he heard the static of the man speaking through the radio and it didn't take a genius to know that he was sending off a warning, putting everyone on alert, just in case something popped off with Queen.

"What's up, Trigga?"

Dre was the first one to greet him, standing at the door, his body positioning himself in a way to block Trigga from walking inside. Trigga peeped the move right off and knew Dre was protecting his wife; wanting to assess Trigga's demeanor for himself before giving him access.

"Ain't shit," Trigga replied. "Listen, I'ma be honest with you, Dre. This ain't no good meeting, but you know I ain't stupid."

Dre's brows hooked over his eyes in a frown for a second before a light passed through them. He knew exactly why Trigga was here and he couldn't fault him one bit because Dre knew, had it been him, he would have been stepping to Trigga the same way. Still, inside the room sat the woman he loved more than life itself, and he wouldn't allow his friendship or respect for Trigga to make him slip.

"I need to search you before you walk in here."

Trigga stepped back and frowned, swatting Dre's hand away. "What da fuck for? I know your team told you that he already checked my ass. I don't appreciate this shit, Dre. I been workin' with yo' ass since we was fuckin' kids! You hired *me* to protect Queen in the first place."

Dre nodded his head with a blank expression on his face. Trigga was correct in what he was saying. When Queen was just starting out, he'd pulled Trigga in to be her personal protector because he was so skilled at what he did. Trigga stayed in that position for several years before he finally decided to go on his own.

"I hear what you're saying, but it is what it is. If you wanna go in to see my wife, I'm going to have to check you myself."

With a heavy sigh, Trigga lifted his hands and allowed Dre to search him for anything that he could use as a weapon, before standing up and stepping back.

"Go ahead," Dre told him, blowing out a sigh of his own.

As soon as Trigga walked in, his eyes fell on Queen who was sitting behind her desk, which was nothing abnormal, but her red-rimmed, puffy eyes and trembling bottom lip gave him pause. This was not what he had been expecting. Dre closed the heavy door behind them and Trigga heard him sigh and walk up behind him. Turning slightly, Trigga cut his eyes at Dre, noticing that he had positioned himself directly behind him. It wasn't until Trigga took a seat that Dre took his as well, a little distance away to allow Queen and Trigga the space to speak.

Queen wiped at her eyes and then opened her mouth to say something. Trigga clamped his mouth closed and prepared to listen.

"Trigga, I'm sorry. I—"

"Are you workin' with that nigga Austin? That nigga attacked my fuckin' wife! He almost killed Keisha and our baby. He *kidnapped* Cam. Tell me you ain't have shit to do with that, Queen!"

Frowning, Queen looked at him with her face screwed tight in a mixture of repulsion as well as confusion.

"How dare you even insinuate that I would have *anything* to do with anyone hurting Cam!" she spat at him with a tone as potent as the venom in a snake.

"Cam?! What about Keisha?! And if you fuckin' around with his mother, you don't think that shit will affect her fuckin' son? You can't be that stupid!"

To his side, Dre sat up and cleared his throat, but Trigga ignored him. He'd sat back and allowed his wife to play games with his family for months, so if it didn't mean suicide, Trigga would have placed a bullet in both of their skulls.

"You need to watch your tone and remember your place," Queen spat, her eyes gleaming with the serious intent in her words. "I have never worked with Austin in any capacity. I wouldn't allow anyone to lay a hand on Keisha or Cam. The only person I've spoken with and made deals with concerning you was Lania. And my request was simple." She shrugged nonchalantly as if she weren't talking about how she requested that a bitch do her best to fuck up Trigga's entire life.

"I told her to cause a little rift between the two of you so you would let this Mr. Roger's shit you've been doing go. If Keisha loved you like she said she did, she wouldn't have never made you change. She wouldn't have forced you to have no ties with anything dealing with your past. Even the dumbest of hustlers know that you make enemies in the streets that never go away even if you try to leave the block. That's why you always keep an ear to the ground. She weakened you and—"

Trigga was tired of hearing the bullshit.

"Don't try to make this shit seem like you did it because of me, because we both know you don't give a fuck. This was about you not having a replacement for a nigga like me. Be honest."

Queen's eyes darted from Trigga's face to Dre who shrugged in response.

"That is partially true," she admitted. "But as a friend, I could see you weren't happy, your business was suffering, and you were making dumb ass decisions to cover your mistakes. Your marriage would have ended anyways."

"But had you allowed it to end naturally, you would have gotten what you wanted and we still would have been able to keep whatever the fuck kinda relationship this is that we've got," Trigga said in a calm voice, knowing there was no point in sitting here any longer. He'd gotten the information he needed.

"Don't fuckin' call me 'bout no other bullshit," he continued, and Queen's eyes grew wide. "Any business we had is over. I ain't doin' shit for you ever again, and you need to leave me and my family alone."

Reaching out, Trigga knocked his knuckles twice on the top of her mahogany desk and then stood to leave. Dre stood as well to walk Trigga to the door without saying a word. As a man, he understood where Trigga was coming from. He'd even told Queen that she was wrong in meddling with someone else's life, especially someone as key to them as Trigga but, as usual, she thought she had it all figured out.

Pow! Pow!

Blocka! Boom!

Rat-a-tat-a-tat-a-tat-a-tat-a-tat!

"What the fuck?!" Trigga and Dre both said at the same time.

From the sound of it, a vicious gun battle had ensued. It sounded like the next World War had begun. By habit, Trigga reached to his side for his gun before realizing that he'd hidden it elsewhere because he was aware of the pat down he'd receive from Queen's men. Shifting a little, he reached down his front and grabbed the small gun that he'd kept secured against his left thigh. Positioning it in his hand, he checked the bullets and took off the safety. When he looked up, he noticed Dre's probing eyes on him.

"I'on never go nowhere without my piece on me. Believe that shit," he said and then tore his eyes towards the door as the gunfire continued.

"You're gonna need something better than that," Dre told him and led him to a closet to their right.

When he opened the door, there were weapons on weapons on weapons, all laid out on the table with rounds of bullets to match each one. There was also protective armor. Trigga and Dre both put one on before Dre ran out to help Queen into hers as she analyzed the computer screens at her desk. Her eyes were wide and her mouth was formed into a perfect circle as she saw her men shooting and being shot right on her own property.

Thankfully, their children were visiting Dre's mother that weekend because from the looks of it, she wasn't sure how they would make it out alive. Whoever was attacking them had come prepared and wasn't letting up a bit.

On the other side of the massive building that Queen called her home, was Austin, smiling wide, like the cat that ate the canary, as he watched his team move in on Queen's security crew. Queen took a hit when she allowed Trigga to use her forces to protect his family as well as his club. That meant there were less men protecting hers, and Austin had been banking on that. Still, she had enough niggas patrolling to make up a small army, but Austin's reinforcements had come just in time and they had the element of surprise on their side.

Austin hadn't thought he'd get so lucky and find Trigga so soon, but when Mendoza called him and said that he'd been spotted at his own club, he'd hit the jackpot. Trigga was just as cocky as rumors had him to be. He thought he was untouchable, but that was all about to come to an end.

Austin received the second call from Mendoza about half an hour later and it was the one he'd waited years to receive. After following him, Trigga had led them right to Queen's home as Austin had suspected he one day would. The problem was, her shit was armored like the fuckin' White House. But Austin knew it wasn't nothing that he couldn't work his way through. He'd lose a great deal of men, but it would be worth it in the end.

And here he was. Bodies were dropping like flies, but it included members of her team as well as his so Austin wasn't panicking. Sitting in the back of his all-black Suburban truck, he clutched the AK-47 in his hands and watched the action, his eyes darting back and forth as he looked for an opening to get out the truck and join the battle.

Boom! Boom!

He finally got it when one of his men shot off an AR-15 and blasted about ten of Queen's men at one time. Without hesitating a second longer, Austin jumped out of the back of the truck and ran towards Queen's mansion, heading the opposite direction from where his men were battling it out in the front. He knew enough to know that was the last place he'd find Queen. Surely, Trigga and her husband were trying to find her another means of escape while her men did the dirty work.

"We gotta get her out of here," Trigga mumbled as he continued to listen to the heavy machinery outside, sending off shots like thunder. "We don't have much time."

There was no sound behind him so he turned around, seeing Dre and Queen both staring at the camera screens, watching the slaughter of their men as they waited for the opportune time.

"Now. Let's go," Dre said finally, grabbing his wife's hand. She followed behind him without a single shred of fear on her face. Queen didn't have confidence in many people, but she fully trusted the two men around her when it came to her protection. This wasn't the first time she'd had to put her life in their hands.

As soon as they walked out the door, Dre led them in the opposite direction from the gunfire, further into the house. Trigga followed at the rear, keeping his eyes open for anything or anyone that threatened their path. And then, outside of one of the windows near him, he saw a familiar face.

"Austin," he gritted through his teeth.

Dre and Queen heard him and they both knew what he was about to do. Cupping Queen close to his side, Dre continued running, determined to find a way out for his wife as Trigga followed behind the new object of his pursuit. Using the butt of the gun, Trigga punched hard through the window, shattering the glass before sending off several shots where Austin stood. He ducked to the ground just in a nick of time, and Trigga missed narrowly. Lifting his body up, Trigga slid out of the window quickly, cutting his back in the process with a few stray pieces of glass, and then fell to the ground with his gun up, his eyes darting around for Austin.

Blocka! Blocka!

Austin didn't have a good visual of Trigga, but he had a sense of where he was so he aimed his weapon and pulled tight on the trigger, hoping that one of the shots would land.

Boom!

Trigga fired back in the direction of the bullets that had whizzed by his head. He got a lucky shot in and caught Austin in the shoulder. The pain burned, searing his skin like a piece of raw meat, and Austin gritted his teeth together to stop himself from crying out as he lay back against a tree. His body told him to leave but his mind wouldn't let him. He knew this was his final chance to get Queen. He wouldn't be given an opportunity like this ever again. It was now or never.

Jumping out from behind the tree, Austin delivered several more shots in a maniacal fashion, eager to just be done with Trigga altogether so he could get to his prize before she escaped. He knew the longer he waited, the more time Queen had to find a hiding place that he wouldn't be able to infiltrate. But Trigga stayed as poised as ever, knowing that desperation was the reason for a lot of niggas' downfalls.

Squinting his eye, he looked around the shed that he was positioned behind and saw that he had a clear shot to Austin's arm as he lay behind a tree, breathing heavily as he pressed hard against a shoulder wound on the same arm. Trigga aimed and shot—*Boom!* Austin let out a loud wail as his arm separated from his shoulder, bits of it flying in the opposite direction. Now it was time for Trigga to finish the job. Standing up, he began to walk towards Austin as the man continued to wail for the arm he'd lost. Never in Trigga's life had it felt *this* good to end a life. Except maybe when he was ending Austin's cousin's.

Blocka! Bloom!

Rat-a-tat-a-tat-tat!

Trigga dove for cover as shots erupted from behind.

"What da fuck?!"

Clutching the ground, he army crawled while holding his gun until he was able to get underneath a piece of debris that had fallen. It wasn't much, but he was able to hide just in time as he saw a group of Austin's men flood onto the scene.

"Shit! The boss been hit! We gotta get him outta here. Fuck!"

Fuck! Trigga thought as he watched the group surround Austin, looking out with their guns raised as four of them grabbed him up and hoisted him between them, carrying him hastily as he wailed out in pain.

Biting down hard on his bottom lip, he considered firing at Austin still, thinking that even with his men surrounding him, he may get off a lucky shot. But so far, luck had not been on his side. After that, his next thought was Keisha, Cameron, and their unborn child. He had to make it home to them. By the time Trigga was able to safely remove himself from under the debris, Austin and his men were gone. But Trigga knew with Austin severely weakened, his days were numbered.

26

*T*rigga was back in his office at his club, the same place he'd been at for the past few days, plotting and making plans.

Since the moment he entered the club, Lania had been dying to get him alone so she could say something to him. She wanted to get a vibe as to where they stood. She needed to know if she still had a chance but, from the moment that he entered his office, he rarely left other than to go into the adjoining room that held his personal shower and restroom. After asking around the club, she realized that he hadn't even eaten a thing since he'd been in there.

According to Choice, who had heard a few things from her 'sources,' everything wasn't well between Keisha and Trigga at home and that was part of the reason he wasn't going back. Lania smirked to herself when Choice told her it had something to do with Keisha finding the thong that Lania had planted there. Even with the little mishap between them a few days ago, Lania's plan was still in effect.

After dancing on stage for the second time that night, an encore performance requested by one of the V.I.P. guest, Lania finally received the message she was waiting on.

"Aye, Nia," Choice called out, and Lania knew from the shit-eating grin on her face that she either had good gossip or she was up to something. "The boss wanna see you in his office."

"Me?" Lania pushed for further clarification while pressing her fore-finger into her bare chest.

"Yes you, bitch," Choice replied before licking her lips and giving her a little wink. "Don't do nothing I wouldn't do."

"I intend to do *everything* your ass would do if you had the chance. And more..." Lania teased before tying her thin top back on to cover her nipples. She would have normally gone in naked, but knowing what she knew about Trigga, she could get further with him by playing coy.

"Ohh bitch, I knew y'all was fuckin'!" Choice squealed and Lania didn't move to correct her. She wanted that kind of gossip going around. By the time Lania had even made it to Trigga's office, Choice had already told three girls that Lania was the one Keisha had kicked him out of their home over.

Lania knocked lightly on the door before walking into Trigga's office. He was standing up with his back turned to her but spun around slowly as soon as she entered in. Not saying a word, he watched her slip in the room, closing the door shut behind her, before bringing her beautiful light brown eyes to meet his. Trigga stared into them and wondered how many men she'd brought to their knees with one simple look. She was a beautiful woman.

"You asked for me?" Lania replied to which Trigga nodded his head.

He gestured for her to sit in the chair in front of his desk and she did as asked. But instead of Trigga sitting in his own chair behind the desk, he came to her side and positioned himself on top of the desk, directly in front of her. Lania's eyes fluttered as she sucked in the scent of his heavy cologne and when she opened her eyes again, she couldn't help but let her pupils fall to the center of his crotch and admire the bulge. She licked her lips as her mouth began to water. It was hard to pay attention to anything else with him seated right in front of her face, but she found a way to look up into his face.

"It's no secret my wife and I are having problems. And I know the last time we spoke I was a little hard on you..."

Pushing herself not to look down at Trigga's dick when he shifted in front of her, Lania nodded her head and kept her eyes on his.

"I—I didn't want to come between you two, I was just desperate because Queen was helping me. She gave me money to help with my kids."

"I know, but I'm not worried about that shit. I just thought that every-thing going on between us... how you make it seem like you feelin' a nigga... I thought all that was a joke to you. A game that you were bein' paid to play."

Frowning, Lania started to stutter as she eagerly began to set the record straight.

"N-n-no! That wasn't it at all. I *am* feelin' you. I think I love you... but I knew that with you bein' with her—with Keisha—that I didn't have a chance, so I've been tryin' to keep my distance and just let things play out however. But you know, she was cheating on you so..."

The wheels in Lania's mind began to work as she saw how she could twist this inquisition for her own benefit.

"Once a cheater, always a cheater. She's not goin' to change, Trigga. But me, I only want you. Nothing Queen told me to do made me fake my feelings for you. Are you still with your wife? I noticed you've been here the past few nights."

"Fuck her," was Trigga's immediate response. "She found some thong in my pants that probably belong to her and kicked me out the house. But I was gonna leave anyways because I'm sick of the fuckin' pressure. No matter what da fuck a nigga does, it's never enough for a bitch—"

"But you've always been enough for me!" Lania stood up and pressed her body between Trigga's legs, not able to ignore the bulge of his dick any longer. She positioned herself on top of it and when she heard him groan, it set her entire body on fire.

"Am I?" he asked and she nodded her head before kissing the tattoos on his neck.

Reaching up, Trigga pinched one of her nipples through the thin material of her top and she gasped, twirling her hips closer to his dick, rubbing her pussy against him.

"You're enough for me too," he told her as he leaned down and ran his tongue down her neck, suckling in between licks. "If only I could rid myself of that bitch."

"Keisha?" Lania asked, jerking her head back to make sure he'd heard her clearly.

"Yeah... she knows too much shit about me. If I left her for you, she would run her fuckin' mouth to the Feds and any other nigga who would listen. If someone would get rid of her ass, it would just be me and you."

Lania's lips parted as she stared into Trigga's eyes, hearing everything he was saying and also understanding the things that he wasn't saying. He wanted her to help him. He wanted *her* to kill Keisha.

"I understand," was her only response.

Standing up, Trigga sighed and turned his back to her as he grabbed up a few things from his desk before turning back.

"I'm goin' out of town for a day or so. I need you to take care of things. The club or... whatever else. Okay? Then me and you can do our thing."

Lania nodded her head slowly, her eyes stretched open wide. She understood exactly what he meant.

IT WAS LATE the next night when Keisha opened her eyes, feeling as though she was being watched as she lay in the bed. She looked at the clock on her nightstand. *3:48* was the time it read. Yawning, she turned her eyes to the ceiling and wondered how long she would be able to live like this, alone and without Trigga. He hadn't been home in days. She hadn't seen him in just as long and, truthfully, she wasn't certain when she would see him again. Years ago, she wouldn't have thought that this would be the reality of their relationship but... here they were.

She stood up and grabbed her robe, wrapping it around her body. Stepping out of her room, she walked down the hall to peek into Cameron's room and then traveled back down the hall, deciding this would be a good time to make herself a pot of *Sleepytime Tea* to aid her in going to sleep. The moment she reached out to turn on the light switch, she heard something go bump in the night and she jumped back, narrowly missing a lamp that came sailing right at her head.

Bam!

The lamp crashed to the floor but before Keisha could react, a body jumped on top of her. The masked figure was dressed in black from head-to-toe and was wielding a large butcher knife straight at her face.

"Ugh!" Keisha grunted, panicking at first before her lessons started to kick in.

She'd prepared for this. Trigga hadn't signed her up for months of kick-boxing for no reason. This was the time for her to perform. Rearing back, she held the knife away with as much force as she could muster with one hand, and then used the other to punch the figure continuously in the neck, hoping to weaken their grasp on the knife.

"Argh!" the assailant screamed out when Keisha was able to successfully twist her wrist up in an unnatural way that was nearly cracking bone. Keisha pushed harder and harder and harder, twisting the arm even more so until she did hear a *snap!* indicating the wrist was broken. Still, the person began to fight, kicking Keisha in her growing belly before reaching out for the knife again.

"Oof!" Keisha grunted, holding her belly as tears stung her eyes.

This is my moment! Lania screamed in her thoughts as she grabbed the knife in her good hand.

The bitch, Keisha, had broken her wrist, probably shattered it, and it hurt like hell, but she was fueled by her hate for Keisha and her love for Trigga. She wasn't going to let one small broken bone stop her. Trigga had asked her to kill Keisha, and that was exactly what she intended to do. Grabbing the knife in her hand, Lania turned around with it high in the air, ready to stab Keisha over and over again; first, right in the heart, and then in the belly to kill the child she had created along with Lania's soulmate, Trigga, the man who would finally be hers forever.

Click!

Lania stopped short and all of the blood drained from her face when she turned around and was met by the barrel of a gun, aimed directly at her. Keisha's eyes were squinted tightly into narrowed slits as she aimed the weapon with confidence, knowing that she was finally about to put an end to Lania's life.

"You fuckin' bitch! Drop the knife and take off the mask," Keisha ordered through her teeth. Lania paused for only a second before dropping the knife down on the floor and ripping the burglar's mask off her face. And then, to Keisha's surprise, she began to laugh. It was an evil, maniacal chuckle. She had lost her mind.

"Put the gun down, Keesh. It's just me... you aren't goin' to kill me, are you?"

Keisha squinted even harder at Lania. Was this bitch crazy? Lania had been trying to kill *her*, what made Lania think that Keisha wouldn't return the same favor back?

"I'm your friend, Keisha!"

"You're not my fuckin' friend! I remember everything!"

Keisha had been in the middle of a kickboxing class the day after she had accused Trigga of cheating on her when her memory returned to her. Because of her worries about her marriage, she'd been off her game and her instructor got a good hit in that she expected Keisha to block. The hit was straight to the skull and Keisha dropped to the mat, struggling to catch her breath as she was flooded with clips of memories that she'd forgotten. It was then that she remembered Lania was not a friend. Not only was she after Trigga, Keisha had also remembered that she was the one who had been meeting with Austin the day that he attacked her. All along that bitch had been playing both sides.

"Oh, you remember, huh? What do you remember?" Lania baited, knowing that there was nothing of worth that Keisha could possibly know except that they weren't friends like she'd tried to lead her to believe. But then Keisha opened her mouth and said something that Lania wasn't expecting.

"I know you've been working with Austin. I know you are behind everything that's been happening with Trigga. The day I was attacked, I *saw* you walk out of the hotel he was in... you were crying. You've been helping him to get to Trigga all along."

Once again, the blood drained from Lania's face but she recovered quickly when she realized that Keisha couldn't possibly have shared her knowledge with Trigga.

"It's obvious that you haven't shared what you know because I spoke with Trigga and he is the reason I'm here," Lania informed her smugly. "He is the one who told me to get rid of you so that he and I can be together."

"Really?" Keisha said, her eyes going wide in disbelief. Lania started to laugh once again, seeing that she had hit Keisha right where it hurt.

"Really. He doesn't want you, probably never did. I mean..." She pointed at Keisha. "Look at you and then look at me." She outlined her frame with her hands. "He personally asked me to kill you."

"Oh," Keisha replied quietly, nodding her head as she looked down. Lania took a step forward feeling like this was her time to act, but then, suddenly, Keisha lifted her head and a malicious smile of her own crossed her face.

"Well, just know that the man you think you love—the one who told you to kill me—is the same one who helped me set this up so that I could kill you."

Pow!

Lania's eyes widened and she looked down, stunned, as she stared at the bloody red hole in her side. But Keisha wasn't done. She treated Lania's body like a target that she'd aimed at many times during practice with Rodney, and continued shooting.

Pow! Pow! Pow!

After the final shot rang through the air, Lania's body dropped, her eyes still stretched open wide and her mouth in a perfect circle as if she was about to say something. But it was too late. Her life was gone.

Keisha let out a breath and then grabbed her cell phone out of her robe, the same robe where she'd had her gun stashed. She pressed a button and then placed the phone to her ear.

"It's done," she said as soon as Trigga answered the phone.

"Already?"

Keisha giggled, rolling her eyes. "Whatever. I told you that I could handle this. Thank you for letting me. I'm glad you let me help you. I needed this."

Her eyes filled with tears but she blinked them away. It had taken forever to convince Trigga to let her take care of Lania on her own but she was happy that he'd trusted her to hold her own. With everything going on, she needed to prove that she was a real part of Trigga's team. And she needed to prove to him that he didn't have to worry; she could take care of herself.

"I love you," was Trigga's response and it warmed her heart. "Dre said he'll arrange for the clean up and also drop Cam off to you tomorrow, or they can even keep him a few more days if you want to relax. I'm about to jump on the plane now that I know you're good, and the next time you see me, this will all be over."

"I know it will."

27

*A*ustin winced as he reached over to grab up his glass of Henny and then downed it all in one big gulp. One day he would wake up out of this state of depression that he'd found himself in. One day. But as for now, he was ready to drink his life away. Not only had he failed at taking over Queen's empire, but Trigga had blown off his entire fuckin' right arm. Although he hadn't shown his face in Texas since he flew in directly into his backyard, word traveled fast and everyone knew that the boss wasn't the boss they had once highly regarded. He was a cripple. He'd lost his shooting arm and now even needed a nurse to wipe his own ass.

"You want me to update you on what's goin' on?" J.D. asked as he sat at Austin's side, the edge of his lip flinching as he tried to hold back his smile. He couldn't say that he was upset that Austin had come into contact with the wrong side of Trigga's gun. Since Karmen, may her soul rest in hell, had poisoned his mind against him, whether Austin found merit in her words or not, he'd demoted J.D.'s position to virtually nothing.

It wasn't until he came back home and saw that his entire empire had been going to shit since he'd removed J.D. from being in charge that he asked for him back. But by then it was too late. J.D. understood that his long tenure of loyalty under Austin, his dedication and his friendship didn't mean shit to him, and it never had.

"I don't give a fuck about what's goin' on! You just handle that shit, nigga. If you wanna be in charge, be in fuckin' charge when I need you to. Stop actin' like you gotta run every damn thing by me. I got enough shit to worry about," Austin spat, slurring his words. "DEENA!"

Moments later, a woman walked in, seductively swishing her hips and ass from side-to-side. But her eyes weren't on Austin, as they normally were, but on J.D. instead. She knew that he would be the new leader and she was already in line to stake her claim. Austin was going to continue to drink himself into a stupor; it was obvious from how he'd spent the last few days. Plus, she didn't want to be stuck wiping his ass for the rest of his life because it was obvious he was not trying to learn how to take care of himself on his own.

"Somethin' wrong wit'cha fuckin' eyeballs, bitch?! I'm the nigga who called you." Austin gritted his teeth, annoyed that he was no longer the most sought-after nigga in the room. J.D. half-smiled behind his back.

"How can I help you, Mr. Austin?" she asked with sarcasm. She wasn't even afraid of him anymore. He just seemed so fake and flawed, plus, he was acting like a spoiled brat.

"Get me another fuckin' drink! And hurry."

Rolling her eyes, she sighed and then took off in the opposite direction. She was tired of his antics. When he first employed her as his housekeeper, she saw the job as a means to an end. They'd fuck every now and then and she'd clean up afterwards, telling herself that one day he'd make her his woman. Now, she wasn't interested at all. As soon as her shift was over and she got her next check, she was going to leave this fuckin' job.

"Da fuck you still sittin' there for, you smilin' ass nigga? Go out and run my shit!" Austin fumed and then turned to grab his glass of Henny before remembering that Deena hadn't brought it back yet. "Shit! DEENA!"

Two seconds after he called Deena's name, he heard the sound of glass crashing to the floor followed by the fast-paced clicking sound of heels on the tile, as if she were running away.

"Da fuck?!" Austin sat up in his seat as much as he could, using one arm, and peered down the hall where she'd disappeared. He could hear the heavy thumps of stomping coming towards him. Swiveling fast, he almost fell over on his side when he turned to look at J.D., his eyes opened wide.

"Get da fuck up! Somebody in here!"

But J.D. didn't move and it was then that Austin swallowed hard, knowing that he'd been betrayed.

"We meet again. How's the arm?"

Closing his eyes, Austin knew these were his final moments as soon as he heard Trigga's voice. He'd come to kill him. It was the end and Trigga had won. Turning around once more, he looked into Trigga's steely gray eyes and then Gunplay's menacing brown ones. In their hands, they were each holding weapons and at their feet were two militant and muscular Doberman Pinscher dogs that were licking their chops and looking at him like he was a gourmet meal. Austin shivered, knowing right then that Trigga and Gunplay were not going to bless him with an easy death.

"We ain't come to talk, Trigga," Gunplay sneered with a curled lip and Trigga nodded his head.

"Indeed. We didn't."

"Zeus... Athena! *Essen!*" Gunplay hissed and the dogs obeyed, running towards Austin to rip him to shreds. The sound of their growls and teeth gnashing as they ripped his skin was all that could be heard as the feasted on his body. Austin opened his mouth to yell but one of the dogs, the female, jumped up and bit down on his lips, tearing them straight from his skull.

"Halt!" Gunplay ordered and the dogs stopped instantly, backing away from Austin's near-corpse as he wheezed and struggled to let out breaths. Chunks of his flesh were missing but he was still hanging on, although he would soon succumb to his injuries and die in a matter of seconds, Trigga wanted to be the one to actually take away his life.

Lifting his gun in the air, Trigga aimed it right at Austin's partially-chewed chest and placed his finger against the trigger. Austin closed what was left of his eyes, waiting for his life to flash before his eyes but, for some reason, the last image he saw was of Lania and their children. He gritted his teeth in what would have been a smile, had his lips been intact, just as the first bullet ripped through his flesh.

Zip! Zip! Zip!

Trigga fired three shots from his fired weapon right into Austin's heart, and he was dead instantly. There were no mistakes made in this moment; his dead body lay there as evidence.

"It's done," Gunplay said before walking over to stare down at Austin's mutilated body. He kicked at his legs a few times before grunting content-edly. Still, he couldn't resist coming that whole way and not even getting to fire a single shot. Lifting his gun, he pumped three bullets of his own into Austin's chest.

Zip! Zip! Zip!

"Now you really dead, muthafucka."

Snickering at Gunplay's crazy antics, he turned to J.D., who looked sick in the face, and gave him a curt nod before walking over to dap him up and then pulling him into a half-hug.

"Thanks for the tip, man."

"Don't mention that shit. I had my own bone to pick with Austin, but when he told me to kill his own fuckin' kids, I had to draw the line at that."

Trigga's brows shot up in the air. "You ain't kill no babies, right, nigga?"

"*Hell* naw," J.D. replied. "I told him I did so he'd stop lookin' for 'em, but I hid them. Set 'em up nice in a house in Atlanta."

"Take care of them," Trigga told him. "They done lost both of their parents."

J.D. nodded his head without saying a word, even though inwardly he wasn't happy to hear of Lania's demise. He had a soft spot for her but he also knew that, whatever happened, she'd brought it upon herself.

"So this your empire now! If a nigga ever swing through, just break bread with my ass. Don't act like you don't know me, a'ight?" Gunplay chuckled as he dapped J.D. up as well. J.D. returned it with a frown.

"*My* empire?" he chirped. "I thought since y'all killed his ass that you would be takin' over."

Shaking his head, Gunplay ran his hands through his long dreads. "Hell naw, I got enough waitin' for me in New York. Plus..." He looked at Trigga. "I have a new partner in crime. We workin' together for life now, right, B?"

Blowing out a burst of air through his nose, Trigga paused a bit before finally nodding his head. After years of being without a partner since he lost his twin brother, Trigga was finally ready to work as a team again.

"Yeah, we can be in discussion 'bout that shit," Trigga replied, not wanting to give in so easily. Gunplay twisted up his lip and shook his head.

"See, here you go wit' that bullshit, Trigga."

Laughing, Gunplay playfully punched Trigga in the arm and they walked out, talking back and forth about how it would be to work together as a team.

Maybe one day.

EPILOGUE

"If you look really close, you can see the baby kicking," Keisha said to Trigga as they stared at her huge belly. She was nearly to term now and in a matter of weeks, they would be welcoming in a new baby girl.

"Kicking with her little bitty web toes," she added, joking as she referenced a trait that both Trigga and their son shared.

"Fuck outta here," Trigga laughed, nudging her lightly.

So much had changed in their lives, but now that it was over, Trigga found that the bad things worked out for the good. Although he was no longer working with Queen directly, he still picked up favors that Dre requested of him. Trigga was no dummy, he knew that Dre was only the go-between between Trigga and his wife, but Trigga couldn't bring himself to cut Queen off completely, no matter how much pain she'd almost caused him. He knew that she wasn't the type of woman to repeat her errors, so he had no doubt that she'd learned her lesson and would never interfere in his personal life again.

Although Trigga still had the club, he had someone else in charge, a young cat by the name of Gunner, whom he'd almost hired just based off his name. With Gunner in charge, Trigga was able to use the club to launder the money that he made in the streets. Gunner was a young, charming cat that the ladies loved and the niggas respected, but he was also smart as hell with a keen business sense. The club was making so much money that Trigga was contemplating on buying The Gentleman's Club and a few other spots he'd peeped in the area.

His home life was perfect, even though he spent many nights away working on business for Queen or working with Gunplay. His marriage was strong as ever and Keisha was the perfect life companion. She managed his books, becoming more involved in his street deals than she had in the past. Instead of ignoring what he did for a living and pretending like that part of him didn't exist, she learned to appreciate every bit of him and find places where she could make life easier for the both of them.

"Do you want to have another after this one?" Keisha asked, failing at biting down her smile. Trigga lifted one brow and cut his eyes at her.

"Hell naw. Let's just get this one out the way first. Hell, if she cries as much as Cam did, we might give her ass away."

Giggling, Keisha rolled her eyes and cuddled in close to Trigga, lacing her fingers through his. She felt absolute contentment in his arms. Thinking back to the question LeTavia had posed about whether or not she ever felt like she needed 'alone time,' she was satisfied in knowing that her answer was still the same: no. She never wanted to be apart from Trigga. But she wondered if he felt the same. Twisting her face up so that she could look into his eyes, she decided to ask.

"Do you ever feel like you need time away from me, just to like clear your mind or..." She paused, trying to find the right words to correctly illustrate her point. Trigga didn't need her to continue.

"No," he replied emphatically, as if there was nothing else in the world that was truer than the word he'd spoken. He peered deeply into her eyes, probing through them so far until it felt like he was speaking directly from his heart into hers.

"If I could spend every single minute of my life around you—*in* you..." She blushed behind her beautiful caramel skin, ducking her head down, but Trigga lifted her face by placing a single finger under her chin.

"If I could be with you every second of the day and never leave your side, I would." He finished and then released her at the exact moment that she felt her sex began to throb. "If I could fuck you all day, suck between your legs until you passed out from pleasure, smell the sweet scent of your pretty pussy on my lips until you couldn't take it anymore—"

Keisha groaned, feeling like she was about to explode just from his words.

"—I would."

By this time, Keisha was squeezing her thighs together as she breathed evenly, trying to keep herself under control, when all she really wanted was to straddle her husband and ride him into ecstasy.

"I'm hungry as fuck," Trigga said and Keisha's eyes opened. She frowned slightly, pouting once she realized that they wouldn't be playing out all of the nasty things that had just come from his mouth.

"I'll make you somethin'. I just cooked some—"

Before she could finish, Trigga plunged two fingers under her short nightgown and right into her sopping wet pussy, spreading her lips as he ran them back and forth over her clit. Keisha gasped and let out a long breath as he continued massaging her. She gushed on his fingers and opened her legs wider as he continued to probe her before pulling his fingers out and then dipping them into his mouth.

"Mmm," he moaned as he noisily slurped and licked his fingers, lapping up her juices from his fingers. Keisha watched him, feeling herself become more and more aroused.

"Naw, I think this will do!"

And with that, Trigga lifted her up, picking her straight up off the couch like she weighed no more than a feather, like she wasn't carrying a whole baby inside of her, and began to carry her towards the room.

"Trigga!!" Keisha giggled, kicking her feet when he started tickling her with his fingers from behind.

"That's my shit, Keesh. Stop buckin' when we could be fuckin'," he joked in the same way he had many times before, and Keisha couldn't stop laughing at how crazy he was.

Their life couldn't get any better.

FROM LEO & PORSCHA

Thank you for reading and we hope you enjoyed this series! Please leave a review. We read, appreciate and love to see them!

NOTE FROM PORSCHA & LEO

Thank you for reading and we hope you enjoyed this series! Please leave a review. We read, appreciate and love to see them!

Porscha & Leo

MORE GUNPLAY & LETAVIA!

Want to learn more about Gunplay & LeTavia? Read 'Shawty Want a Thug' now!

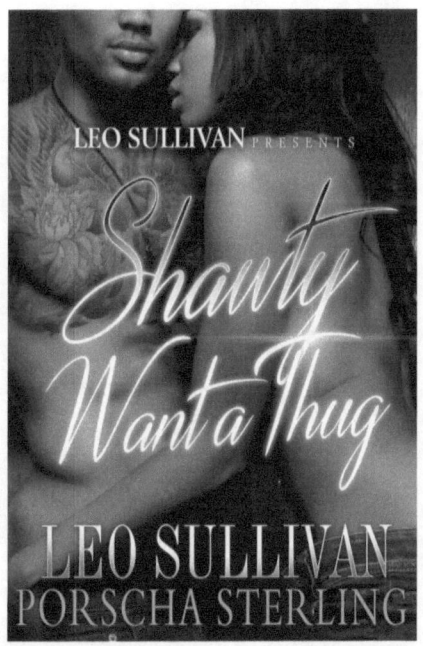

READ MORE ON THE LIT READING APP!

Read more books like this one **for less**! Check out some other new releases on the LiT Reading App. Go to www.litreadingapp.com to learn more!

JOIN OUR MAILING LIST!

Text **LEOSULLIVAN** to **22828** to join our mailing list!
To submit a manuscript for our review, email us at
submissions@leolsullivan.com

To submit a manuscript for our review, email us at
leosullivanpresents@gmail.com